RAVAGED

WITH **YOU**

J. KENNER

NEW YORK TIMES BESTSELLING AUTHOR

Also By The Author

STARK SECURITY
shattered with you
shadows of you-short story
broken with you
ruined with you
wrecked with you
destroyed With You
memories of You (novella)
ravaged With You
charmed By You

THE STARK SAGA
novels
release me
claim me
complete me
anchor me
lost with me
enchant me

novellas
take me
have me
play my game
seduce me
unwrap me

deepest kiss

entice me

hold me

please me

indulge me

cherish me

visit www.jkenner.com for a full list of titles

Praise for J. Kenner's Novels

"*Shattered With You* is a sultry little page turner that comes brimming with scorching passion, edge of your seat action, and heart-wrenching emotion." *Reds Romance Reviews*

"J. Kenner is an exceptional storyteller. The drama, tension, and heat were perfect." *About That Story*

"PERFECT for fans of *Fifty Shades of Grey* and *Bared to You*. *Release Me* is a powerful and erotic romance novel." *Reading, Eating & Dreaming Blog*

"I will admit, I am in the 'I loved *Fifty Shades*' camp, but after reading *Release Me*, Mr. Grey only scratches the surface compared to Damien Stark." *Cocktails and Books Blog*

"It is not often when a book is so amazingly well-written that I find it hard to even begin to accurately describe it . . . " *Romancebookworm's Reviews*

RAVAGED
WITH **YOU**
J. KENNER

M&O

ACKNOWLEDGMENTS

Special thanks to Jessn and Charlie (two awesome tour guides) and the entire staff at Garrison Brothers Distillery in Hye, Texas. The tour was fabulous, the information awesome, and the bourbon even better!

I learned a ton about distilling whiskey, and all errors and liberties taken are my own!

PROLOGUE

He wasn't supposed to be the one. This man who watches me with sensual, luminous eyes, his hair like a crown of fire. This battle-scarred warrior who so tenderly holds my life in the palm of his hand.

My life ... and, yes, my heart.

So many lost years hang between us, along with the weight of so many bad choices, each a scar on my soul. And yet when I look in his eyes and see those dark and haunted shadows, I can't help but think that mine was the easier burden.

Now tragedy and danger draw us together, but we can't ignore the electricity that crackles around us. And that is an altogether different kind of peril.

I'm not a fool; I know I can't have him forever. And I fear that his scars have hardened his heart too much to ever completely let me in.

But as we scramble day after day to stay one step ahead of our enemy, I can't deny one simple truth: I only feel truly safe and happy when I'm in the warm, protective circle of his arms.

CHAPTER ONE

"Hey, Mel, I'm here. Sorry I'm late." Charlie "Red" Cooper paused in the doorway of the Swift Red Distillery's public tasting room and breathed in deep. God, he loved this place. The look of it, all wood and steel and glass. The handcrafted bar he'd tooled and polished himself. The fixtures he'd chosen after countless hours in the Pacific Design Center.

And, oh, the scent of it, that enticing aroma of fine whiskey. Wonderfully heady, and all the more appealing because the place belonged to him.

Well, part of it did, anyway. He and Mel Swift, his best friend since high school, ran the place. And the two of them owned it together with Mel's wife, Jo, the third member of their three-pronged friendship that had started back in college.

Was it only two years ago that they'd celebrated

the distillery's grand opening? Now, Red could hardly imagine any other life. Which, considering he woke up each morning trying to forget the past, was something else in the distillery's favor.

He frowned, suddenly uneasy, those long ago days creeping up on him like shadows. *Back it down. It's nothing.*

He took a breath, then another, all the while cursing himself for opening the damn door in the first place. The door to the dark place where the memories lived. The past. His subconscious. Whatever the fuck the shrink-of-the-week wanted to call it.

Red just called them flashbacks, and those memories had no business here. He might have been the one who'd opened the door, but now he was damn well shutting it again.

"Mel? Hey, buddy, where are you?" He moved through the tasting room as he called, then pushed through the swinging doorway that led to his and Mel's private offices. "You back here?"

Silence. Red frowned, then shot his buddy a text. He waited for the three dots that signified an impending reply, but the screen stayed stubbornly blank.

His frown deepened, then he sighed, shaking his head as reality struck him. *Of course.* He should have gone straight to the distillery. Red loved the business as much as his partner did, but to Mel, it wasn't about the public-facing side, but the magic that turned grain into drinkable alcohol.

In contrast, Red got off on the knowledge of what they'd accomplished. That the public came in, tasted their bourbon, and bought their own bottles to take home. They'd built a business from nothing and had made a drink from grain and chemistry. It was enough to make a man giddy.

Still, he should have known that when Mel said to meet him at work, he didn't mean the public tasting room or even their private offices. What he meant was the solid oak table he'd set up in the rickhouse where he could sit and peruse the books or do paperwork while surrounded by white oak barrels full of aging bourbon.

Now confident he knew where to find his partner, Red headed through the tasting room's back door and toward the huge, corrugated steel building where the real magic happened.

They'd lucked into the property. A former prop warehouse for a company that had supplied to the studios back in the heyday of Hollywood, its location on Santa Monica Boulevard near the Hollywood Forever Cemetery meant they had a lot of walk-in customers, both locals and tourists.

Best of all, the property consisted of two separate buildings. The front was where the original owners had showcased their various props and set pieces. The back building was a warehouse in which they'd manufactured everything from period-specific furniture to crazy hotrods for seventies-style action movies. Back then, it had been one huge space, but Mel and Red had subdivided it into the various rooms that aligned with the distillation process.

A small dirt area separated the two buildings. Or it had until Red spent a full month converting the space into a garden paradise, complete with outdoor seating for guests, along with a secondary bar.

Now, he walked the flagstone path from the public area to the actual distillery. It was a journey he'd taken hundreds—probably thousands—of times since they'd bought the place, and yet he never stopped enjoying it. The way the area smelled of flowers and fruit trees. The way it looked with the stone tables and the fire pit.

It was calming, and God knew that calm had been what he'd been looking for when he'd come back to Los Angeles. He'd needed peace after the hell he'd experienced in Romania.

Not now. Just back it down, buddy.

Red's body tensed from the rising memories, his blood pounding harder in his veins.

Don't go there. Just chill. Think of sunshine and the beach and puppies so goddamn adorable it's a wonder they don't melt in the rain from their sugary sweetness.

Anything. He needed to think about anything other than those years.

Like, for example, catching up to his elusive partner.

With a sharp tug, he pulled open the main door to the distillery and stepped over the threshold and into the rickhouse with its racks of aging bourbon and rye, including Cooper's Slow Burn Rye. A great label, if Red did say so himself.

He saw Mel's table right away, a few papers scattered on top, held down by one of the Swift Red paperweights that Jo had given each of them as a grand opening present.

Mel, however, was nowhere to be found. And he still hadn't answered Red's text.

Again, Red reminded himself that he was the one who'd arrived late, and he set out in search of his partner. He passed through the aisle formed by two racks, then hooked a left toward the long hall that led to the stillhouse. He passed through the series of doors that helped regulate the temperature, then entered the room itself. Immediately, he started sweating, the heat all part of the process.

At first glance, everything in the room looked just fine. The three stills were doing their thing—the Millennium Falcon, the Enterprise, and Firefly. The only thing missing was either Mel or the floor manager, because their number one rule at Swift

Red was to never leave the equipment unmonitored.

Frowning, he checked all the gauges himself, saw that everything was well, then shot off a text to Jessn, the floor manager on the schedule for Monday, the one day of the week they were closed to the public.

You with Mel?

Jessn's reply came quickly: *He gave me the day off. Said he wanted to hang at work and catch up on stuff. I'm at the beach. You didn't know?*

Red's fingers hesitated over the phone, trepidation rising. But all he wrote was, *Crossed-wires. It's fine. Have fun.*

Crossed-wires indeed...

They'd agreed to always discuss any kind of personnel shift, something Mel clearly hadn't bothered with today. Still, Mel must have had his reasons, and Red was pretty damn anxious to hear them. And since Mel clearly wasn't in the still-house, Red exited the room, then followed the maze of racks to the fermentation room, also set off by a series of halls and doors.

This was the room where yeast was added to the crushed grain and water mixture, then left to ferment in a process that increased the alcohol content, but also released carbon dioxide as a byproduct. Because high levels of the off-gas were potentially deadly, this was the most highly moni-

tored room, with a complex series of vents coupled
with a monitoring system that not only visually
showed the level of the gas in the room, but also
sounded an alarm—and automatically texted all
personnel—whenever anything wasn't within the
proper parameters.

Red had received no such alert and the
building was not rocking from the deafening sound
of an alarm—which was why the fact that the visual
indicator above the door was now showing a
deadly-level concentration in that room scared the
shit out of him.

Immediately, he grabbed an emergency
breathing apparatus from a hook by the door.
There were windows on either side, but as the gas
was invisible, nothing seemed out of sorts, and he
saw no sign of Mel. He pulled down on the lever
designed to evacuate any gas from the room by
increasing the suction from the constantly working
filters while increasing the flow of clean air. An
expert in all the ways a project could get fucked up,
Red had insisted the distillery have safety protocols
even beyond those that were required or typical in
the industry.

He checked the gauges, saw that neither the
filters nor blowers had kicked in. That's when he
aimed his gaze upward and was horrified to see that
the ventilation system had been manually closed.
And now, as he looked around the room at the

floor-based scrubbers, he saw that each and every one of them had been unplugged.

Without hesitating, he donned his mask and rushed into the room. Right away, he plugged in each of the scrubbers, their noise immediately filling the space. He looked around, searching for Mel among the dozen waist-high tubs filled with bubbling mash. Not because they were sitting on heat high enough to boil, but because the yeast was doing its job.

He found no sign of his friend, though. He started to pull out his phone and call, then hesitated. Safety first, and he used the ladder to climb up and manually reopen every air vent.

Next, he went to the control panel, only to see that the alarm had been turned to mute, a feature that required the admin password that only he, Mel, and Jo had access to.

What the hell?

Worried and confused, he pulled his phone out again, then checked the gauge. The level was still too high to take off his mask, but was dropping rapidly. He called anyway, intending to talk through his mask. He anticipated hearing either Mel's voice or his damn voicemail message. Instead, he heard an echoing sound. The distinctive refrain of Willie Nelson's *Whiskey River*.

The song that Mel used as his ringtone. And it was coming from among the maze of tubs.

Something dark rumbled in his stomach, churning there like a living thing. Dread, rising and falling. Teasing and taunting. And before Red even knew that he was moving, he'd walked three lines of the grid of tubs that covered the cookhouse floor. He found Mel's phone in the middle, wedged down near the base of one tub.

And there, marked on the tub's plastic outer wall was scrawled a single word: *Sorry*.

Red's chest tightened, fear stealing his breath. The phone's lock screen showed messages from both him and Jo. And still, there was no sign of Mel.

"No. Oh, no, buddy. Tell me you didn't."

Moving as fast as he could, he raced to the wall where they kept the sterile stir sticks. But this wasn't for stirring. Instead, he returned to the tub, then slowly prodded. And—as he'd feared—he hit something solid before the bottom of the tub.

Carefully, he used the stick to hook the solid thing—*please don't be Mel*—*of course it was Mel*—and ease it up far enough so he could grab the familiar blue shirt with the Swift Red Distillery logo.

Forcing himself to stay calm, he hauled Mel up far enough to check his pulse. It wasn't necessary, though. There was no doubt that his friend and partner was dead.

Despite the urge to pull his friend free, Red

released the body, letting it slide back into the mash. He'd already disturbed the scene, and even though every sign pointed to suicide, Red knew enough about the process to know that there would have to be an investigation.

Suicide. Why the hell had his friend committed suicide?

And why hadn't Red picked up on it? What kind of friend was he that he'd missed the warning signs? Sure, Mel had been acting off lately—tricky negotiations for a hotel supply contract was what he'd said, but Red had known that wasn't all of it. There'd been something else on Mel's mind, but Red had never pushed.

Dear God, he should have pushed...

He'd assumed the troubles were between Mel and Jo. They'd gotten married a few years before the grand opening, and he'd been the best man. Which had been both a pleasure and Red's worst nightmare. Because though he would never tell another soul, and especially not the woman herself, the thought of Jo in another man's bed just about killed him.

A totally ridiculous reaction since he couldn't have her. Hell, he'd pushed her away with both hands.

A woman like Jo deserved better than a guy with Red's fucked up issues. But ridiculous or not, his gut had been in knots the day of the wedding.

And as he stood by his two friends' side while they exchanged vows, Red had felt light-headed from the intensity of emotions warring within him. Blood red jealousy and, surprisingly, bittersweet relief. Because at least Jo would be happy. Something that would never happen if she'd ended up with a guy as screwed up as him.

Except now it looked like Mel had been screwed up, too. Everybody had their weak spots. Their vulnerabilities that could push them over the edge.

He ran his fingers through his hair and told himself to back off and get his shit together. He needed to call the cops and let them do their thing. He needed to call Jo and let her know what had happened.

Bottom line? He needed to put aside his anger and his confusion and his grief. There were things to handle, and he was the man at the rudder.

"Right." He drew in a deep breath, then started to put the phone back where he found it. He stopped cold, though, when it rang, the screen showing no caller ID. He hesitated, but answered it.

"I would say that I'm sorry your friend is dead." The voice was filtered, and Red couldn't even tell if it was a man or a woman. "But I'm not."

"Who the hell—"

"He was a bad man. He made bad choices. He

kept something that didn't belong to him. Something that belongs to me."

He looked around, trying to locate the speaker. They knew he'd found the body, so the person must be watching him. But watching from where?

"I'm listening," he said as he slowly stood up, then walked to the windows that looked out onto the hall.

Whoever was at the other end chuckled. "That would be too easy."

Cameras. But where were they mounted? A quick scan of the room revealed nothing.

"What do you want from me?"

"I thought that would be obvious. I want what belongs to me."

"What are—"

"Keep this phone. If you value your life—or the life of his wife—you won't give it to the police. You'll call them, of course. But you will say it was suicide. An investigation would be most inconvenient."

"What did he take? What is it you want back?"

"In case you didn't know, your partner's phone passcode is 798465. An interesting little number. Almost as interesting as the last video that's saved on his phone. Take a look. And remember—keep the phone. It's our link to you. And, though we found nothing of note, perhaps you can uncover a clue to where your partner has stashed our package."

"If you think—"

"I don't mind killing you, but if you do what I say, I'll forgo my jollies and let you and the little wifey live. If you speak to the cops, though ... if you refuse to help me regain what is mine, I will kill you. But I'll kill her first. Watch the video, Charlie. And don't make your partner's mistakes. Be smarter. I'll be in touch."

The phone went dead, and some of the tension drained from his body. He shot a look at the tub his friend was in, his heart heavy. "Mel, buddy. What the hell did you get yourself wrapped up in?"

He didn't want to, but he knew he had to watch the video. He keyed in the passcode, thankful that his training had cemented the number in his memory.

He found Mel's photos, and the last addition was a video, timestamped just a few hours ago.

Someone thin and dressed head-to-toe in black held Mel by the back of the neck. His partner's body was weak, his efforts to struggle useless. They'd already beaten him, the bastards. More than that, they'd already tampered with the CO_2 scrubbers, allowing gas to accumulate to toxic levels. The assailant was masked. Mel was not.

Then the assailant shoved Mel forward, his

face going into the bubbling, semi-liquid mash. One second. Five. Fifteen. Forty. One minute.

Water rushing. Pulse pounding. Garbled voices. No!

For years, he'd managed to keep those demons at bay. Then New York happened and—

Stop it. You can do this. Just shove the memories away.

Right. He could *do this.*

He drew a breath, then rewound the video to where he'd been. He watched once more, gasping, as the assailant yanked his partner up. His hand went automatically to the knife he always kept in his back pocket, and he tried to calm his heartbeat.

In the video, Mel's head wobbled as he tried to catch his breath in a room that was rapidly filling with poisonous air.

Then he was pushed head down into the mash again. Thirty seconds. A minute. Ninety seconds.

You think you can play the hero? You'll only play the fool.

And then back up to try to breathe, only to find there wasn't any more air on the outside than inside that tub.

Mel? Or Red? Who was it who needed air?

Again and again and again until finally the assailant shoved Mel's limp body all the way over the waist-high lip of the tub. And down he went, the mash sucking him in like quicksand.

Memories crashed through Red's mind. He gasped, dropping the phone as his hand reached for his throat. He couldn't breathe. He couldn't fucking breathe.

He tried to swallow, forcing himself to concentrate as he grabbed Mel's phone and shoved it in his pocket.

Under the water. His lungs squeezing. No air. Needed air.

Gasping, trying to breathe, he pulled out his own phone and dialed 911. He heard himself say that his partner had killed himself. That they needed to send someone. His voice was raw. He had no air. He couldn't hear the operator, only the hollow echo of the water that surrounded him.

Then his legs gave out, and he crashed to the floor. He could still hear the emergency operator talking as his entire world went black.

CHAPTER TWO

Before

Blackness. *Sweet, utter blackness.*

He wanted to stay there. Wanted to get lost in it, to never come out of it.

You have to. It's important.

But why? Why was it important?

He couldn't remember. Didn't know what he was doing or where he was. Hell, he didn't even know *who* he was.

Icy panic flooded his veins, and he bucked, trying to move his hands, then realizing with more astonishment than fear that they were tied behind him.

Where was he? Who was he?

Charlie...

The name was like a whisper in the dark. A

tease. A hint of who he was, or maybe who he had been.

Then a fiery hot sting against his face that seemed to shatter every bone.

"*Again.*"

The harsh word registered on his senses even as another round of fiery blows assaulted his face. Not English, but he understood it. How? How could he understand?

He was here—*but where was here?* He'd been captured—*but by whom?*

More beatings, more pain, more blackness and red pain until something in him seemed to snap and he forced his eyes open and saw his captors. Four tall men, bulky and scarred, and one woman standing behind them, dark hair falling past her shoulders, stunningly beautiful despite a face marred by hatred and disgust.

"Ah, there he is," the woman said, and now he knew. *Romanian.* "We knew that you were in there somewhere, Mr. Cooper."

Memories crashed back. The two flight attendants on a humanitarian mission, training other airline personnel how to detect and help suspected human trafficking victims. And the other woman, a deep-cover SOC agent who'd been taken hostage along with them.

Lisa. The woman he'd been dating on and off for the last two years. A woman whose laughter had reminded him that there was joy in the world despite the horrors he saw in his work.

His work ... Him ... Charlie Cooper.

He'd been assigned to get them out. Him and his team. Now all captured. Now all dead except for him and the women trapped in chains and cages.

It was up to him to save them all.

"You did not think we would kill you, did you? The last man standing? That is some sort of honor, I think. It has bought you time." The woman smiled, a beautiful face on a soul of pure evil. "We will kill you eventually, of course. But not so soon. You have caused us much trouble. We will play before we kill, and you will be sorry for the trouble."

He didn't move. Not so much out of bravery, but because he was tied to a chair. His legs, his arms, his chest. Only his head had any movement at all.

"You will not enjoy this, I think," she said, then nodded to the men. "Though we will."

The men came, two on each side of the chair and lifted him. He was already woozy, and now vertigo hit him dead-on, along with the sickening certainty that he was helpless. This wasn't a movie, and no matter what skills he'd developed during his years of service, they did him no good right now.

If only he had his knife....

With his skill and his fury, he could turn the tables on them. He always carried a blade, but they'd stripped him bare, and the tools he'd had tucked away in pockets and hidden in seams—small but deadly blades, practical lock picks—were long gone now. He wore only the rags they'd clothed him in.

"I *will* kill you," he said, making the woman chuckle.

"Of course you will not. You are not the hero, Mr. Cooper. You are what we call the victim. But not, I think, the first one."

It took a moment for his mind to process what she meant. Then his gaze cut to the women. "No." He swallowed, his mouth entirely dry. "No, don't you dare. They're nothing to you. A nuisance. We both know that their programs haven't done shit to curb your industry."

Not exactly true. There was in fact evidence that the training programs springing up among flight attendants had in fact helped victims. But he wasn't inclined to state actual facts.

"Hush, Mr. Cooper. Enjoy our hospitality. We have prepared a show for you."

As he struggled in his bonds, two of the men pulled one flight attendant from behind a wooden panel. She was naked, her hands tied behind her, her mouth stuffed with a dirty rag.

"Don't." His voice was parched. Cracked.

"Oh, we will. The question is, will you survive to see it? I confess I told a little fib. I want these bitches to understand that they have no champion. You are only a useless man, tied to a chair, and your life is completely within my hands. As is theirs."

He caught Lisa's eyes, saw the fear and horror reflected back at him. He wanted to comfort her, but there was no comfort to be had. The woman was right. A fact she proved again with a wave of her hand.

With no warning, the men flipped the chair over, then took him upside down across the room to a huge barrel with two bars across it. They lowered him, and though he tried to struggle, it was futile. Soon he was suspended head down in the water, the ropes so tight around his waist and chest and legs that he remained immobile as he shook his head and fought not to breathe, not to allow his lungs to suck in, seeking air, air, blissful air. But there was no air to be had, and soon the inside of his head was black, then red. He felt light, lost, and soon he would have no choice but to breathe as his lungs battled to bring him oxygen.

Soon, he would drown.

And then he was up again.

He gasped. Just once, and they started it all over again.

And again. And again.

Until he was choking and spitting. Until his

body trembled and his lungs burned and he was only half-conscious.

"Enough." It was the tallest man who spoke. "You did well. You have bought her a quick death."

And just like that, he pulled a pistol, fired, and that woman—one of the two civilian flight attendants his team had been assigned to rescue—fell dead on the hard concrete floor.

"And now," the woman said, smiling as she stepped closer. "We shall see how the others will die."

No.

No, no, no, no, NOOOOO!

His eyes flew open, and he scooted backward, automatically shielding his face from the next blow.

But there was no blow coming. He was on a concrete floor covered with a layer of waffled plastic squares, the scent of yeast permeating the air.

Not Romania.

Not the woman, not the torture.

He was in Los Angeles. In the distillery.

He sucked in air, yanking his knife from his pocket and clutching it like a talisman as he tried to slow his racing heart and feeling like a goddamn failure for falling down the rabbit hole again after so long without an episode.

Stop it. It was a process. Wasn't that what every therapist he'd seen had said, from government shrinks with high level clearance to the LA doc who'd been all about crystals and cleansing his aura?

The bottom line was that he was strong. He could do this. There was no threat. A body, yes. Memories, hell yeah.

But he wasn't going to get lost in the memories or cower under the strain. They'd broken him, that was for damn sure. But that was seven long years ago, and he'd clawed his way back. It had taken years, but he'd gotten his shit together. And no way was he backsliding now. He could do this.

Hadn't he proved as much in New York? A full-on hostage situation, but he'd held it together. At least until he was alone, anyway.

No one saw the way he'd melted down when he returned to his dad's apartment. The ghosts that haunted him that night. The siren call of one drink, then another and another to soothe those hard edges.

But he'd made it through. He'd done it. Nikki Stark was alive today because he'd taken a bullet intended for her.

He'd survived that hostage situation and he

could do this, too. He had to. For Mel's sake, and for Jo's.

Oh, God. Jo. He still hadn't called her. But he needed to call his brother first.

He sat up, then re-sheathed the knife before tucking it back in his pocket. He checked the other pocket, too, making sure Mel's phone was secured. Then he pushed himself to his feet, thinking about the parameters of the mission he was setting himself on. Identify the perps. Find out what they wanted and obtain it. Arrange an exchange. Then take the fuckers down.

A vague plan, but it would fall into place.

"I'm so sorry, Mel," he whispered toward the tank that had become his friend's tomb. "I know you had some shit going on, but I should have known you wouldn't have taken that way out."

With the goodbye still lingering in the air, he pulled out his phone again. He dialed, holding his breath until he heard the voice on the other end of the line.

"I was just about to call you," his brother Renly said. "Is everything okay?"

"No." Red wasn't going to beat around the bush. Not with Renly, who'd already gotten a vibe. They might not be identical, but the twin thing was real. "Mel's dead."

"Oh, Christ. What happened?"

"Can you get over here? I'm at the distillery."

"Yeah, sure, but—"

"It was suicide, Renly," he snapped, and heard his brother's sharp intake of breath. "Just come. And if Damien happens to be with you, could you drag him along, too?"

"Stark? He's here. But why—"

"Just hurry. Tell him I asked you to bring him. He'll come."

"After the way you saved his wife in New York, he'd buy you the Brooklyn Bridge if you asked. Of course we'll come."

"See you soon—"

"Wait." There was an edge to Renly's voice. Hard, but softened by compassion. "Are you holding up?"

Red hadn't told his brother what had happened in Romania all those years ago, but being Renly, he knew that something had gone down.

"I'm still standing," he said. "Just get here. I need to talk to both of you."

He'd walked while he was talking, and now he was standing in the outdoor area. He could see the interior of the empty tasting room through the wide windows, then realized that he should have locked the damn door. Anyone could have walked in and cleaned them out, even torched the place. He would have lost not only his partner, but his distillery as well. And now it was Jo's distillery, too.

Jo.

Her name filled his head, along with an image of her sweet smile. She still didn't know, and he couldn't keep putting it off.

He dialed her number, dreading the conversation, only to have the call go straight to voicemail. "Jo, it's Red. Give me a call. It's important." He sounded so professional. So in control. But what he felt was numb. *Thank God for his training...*

Since it was Monday, he tried her at work, too, only to be told that she'd taken the day off. "Dammit, Jo. Where are you?"

He tried once more, this time sending only a text. The *whoosh* sound of the send notification still lingered when the front door of the tasting room opened and the authorities stepped in. A medical examiner, a uniformed cop, and a woman he assumed was a plain-clothes detective.

Red drew in one more lungful of fresh air, then entered from the garden to greet them, even though all he really wanted was for them to go away. He wanted time to mourn his friend. Time he didn't have, not when he'd been tasked with finding a mysterious missing package. And certainly not when the caller had specifically said that any punishment for failure would be meted out on Jo.

He just had to hold it together until they left. Then he could track Jo down and find out if she knew anything about the MacGuffin.

He could do that. He drew in a breath, released

it slowly, then marched into the tasting room to meet them.

"Thank you for getting here so fast," he said to the woman who was flashing her badge.

"Detective Amaro. We're sorry for your loss. You told the 911 operator your partner committed suicide?"

"Yes, ma'am." He indicated the door to the distillery. "I can take you back."

She followed with her crew, saying nothing, but with her sharp eyes taking it all in. He showed her the CO_2 scrubbers that had been turned off, the vents that had been closed. He pointed out how the alarm system had been bypassed.

He explained the purpose of the mash tubs and how the fermentation process worked. He showed her the tub in which he'd found Mel's body and explained that he'd left it as he'd found it to aid the investigation.

"And a note?"

He drew a breath, then pointed to the scrawled message written with a Sharpie on the side of the tub.

"Just 'sorry'?" Detective Amaro cocked her head.

He swallowed. "That was it."

"And his behavior recently?"

"He'd been more distant than usual. Closed off. Quiet."

"You weren't concerned?"

"A bit, but when I asked, he just said he had a lot on his mind. He'd been negotiating a hotel contract for us. I think he was putting too much pressure on himself. I should have realized. I should have done something."

The emotion in his voice was real, even if it was murder and not suicide that was causing the thickness in his throat.

"I see," she said, and he wondered if she truly did, especially as she started to walk the area, peering under the tubs, then checking the alarm panel and the lock on the fermentation room door. Red kept his expression bland. The face of a man who simply wanted to put the procedures behind him so that he could mourn his friend.

Entirely true, just not for the reasons he'd shared with Detective Amaro.

Red's phone buzzed. "My brother and a friend just arrived in the tasting room. Do you need me in here?"

"No. But please don't leave. Officer Franklin is in the tasting area. He'll let you know if we need anything further."

"Thanks."

"Mr. Cooper?"

He turned back.

"I'm very sorry for your loss."

He'd been holding it together, but something

about those words from a cop got to him. His throat thickened, and his vision became watery. He managed a nod, then hurried out of the room, wanting nothing more than to disappear into his office for a few moments alone with the memory of his friend.

It didn't happen. Renly and Damien Stark were waiting for him when he reached the tasting room. He and Renly weren't identical, but people often thought they were. Red's hair was brighter, something that had irritated him in school, and he was a few inches taller. Other than that, they might as well have been identical. Now, of course, Red sported a close-trimmed beard and a veritable art collection of tattoos. Renly was clean-shaven, and had only one tat from his time in Special Forces.

Still, they must have looked like a mirror when Renly pulled him into a bear hug. "I'm so sorry, bro. I didn't even know Mel was hurting."

"I know," Red said, breaking away from his brother to take Damien's outstretched hand.

"Whatever you need." Tall and lean, with an athlete's build, the billionaire exuded power and control. And, right now, compassion.

"Appreciate it."

"Did he leave a note? Say anything to you?" Renly exhaled. "I can't wrap my head around it."

"Honestly, I need some air. Let's talk at one of the tables in the garden." He pointed to the bar and the array of whiskey bottles lining the shelves behind it. "Help yourselves. Wouldn't blame you if you needed it."

Renly met his eyes. "Want me to bring you a water?"

"Thanks."

He headed out and the other men soon followed him. For a moment, they just sat silently, Red sipping water as the others sipped whiskey.

He sighed, then lifted his water bottle. "Here's to Mel," he said, and they toasted their friend. "We'll miss you."

As soon as Damien and Renly put down their glasses, Red lowered the boom, his voice pitched low, so it was almost lost in the ambient sounds from nearby Santa Monica Boulevard. Plus, he'd deliberately seated them at the middle table, far enough away from any listening devices or cameras mounted on the walls. "His death makes even less sense than you think."

"What—"

Red leaned in before Renly could finish the questions. "He didn't kill himself," he said, the words barely a whisper. "I'll tell you the rest later, away from here. But it was murder."

"Fuck," Renly said. "That explains why you wanted Damien here, too."

"Because it won't be the police who will be

investigating," Damien said. "It will be Stark Security."

Red met his eyes. "I'm calling in that favor."

"I already told you. Whatever you need," Damien assured him. "I owe you everything. Tell us how he died."

"Woozy from carbon dioxide, then drowned in one of the fermentation tubs."

"Oh, God," Renly said. He focused on Red. "You sure you're handling it?"

Red had never told his brother about what had happened in Romania, but Renly wasn't an idiot, and Red had left a hell of a lot of signposts.

After he left the service and came to California, Red had turned down dates to go diving with his brother, something they'd done for most of their lives in both California and Texas. He even avoided swimming pools. Anything submersive. Or that had the potential to be.

Maybe he'd be fine. But a panic attack in the ocean? Yeah, no thank you.

But Renly didn't know any of that. Not the reason, anyway. But he knew. Somehow, his twin always knew.

"How do you know it wasn't suicide?" Damien asked.

Red glanced purposefully around the court-yard. "For now, you're just going to have to believe me." He may have picked a silent location, but the more he talked, the more he risked being heard.

Technically, he hadn't broken any rules by telling these men it was murder. The voice had said only to keep the truth away from the cops. But Red doubted that his nemesis would care about technicalities.

And it wasn't just listening devices he was trying to avoid. The more he said, the more he risked Detective Amaro catching a whiff. He glanced over to where she now stood on the flagstone path, talking with one of the uniformed officers and someone from the coroner's office.

No, he couldn't risk her learning a thing.

Renly followed Red's line of sight, then swung his leg over the stone bench and stood, nodding toward the detective. "If we're playing evade the cops, I think I'll go see what they know. Or don't know."

"Good luck. She seems the type to hold information close to the vest."

Renly spread his hands. "I don't need luck. It's me." He flashed a grin. "And it doesn't hurt that I know her. Detective Lucia Amaro. She worked a series of ODs on the set of one of the movies I consulted on. Looked like ODs, anyway. Turned out they were murders."

"So you're going to pump her for information?"

Red allowed some welcome humor into his voice. "Should Abby be worried?"

"Never," Renly said, and Red knew he meant it. His brother had been in love with Abby since forever, but never thought he could have her. Now that he did, there was no way that Renly would screw that up.

As Renly headed across the lawn toward the detective, Red took a sip of water, his mind turning to Jo. Immediately, he felt like a complete prick for even letting her inside his head, much less in the context of comparing his love life to his brother's. Except despite whatever other feelings Red had for Jo, she was also a friend. And she was going to need help.

"What?" Damien asked, watching his face.

"I was thinking about Jo," he admitted. "She doesn't know yet."

"You've called?"

"Voicemail. Text. Got nothing." As he spoke, he pulled out his phone and tried again, only to once more get the recording. He held it out to Damien with a sad shrug.

"You'll be there for her," Damien said. "We all will. And Jo's strong."

"She is," Red said, smiling despite the situation. "She always has been. But she shouldn't have to be strong for this."

"No one should," Damien agreed. "I'm glad I

got to meet her and Mel. I would have liked to have known him better."

Red cupped his hands over his chin, feeling the scruff of his beard. He sighed, a sound of utter exhaustion. "To tell you the truth, today I've been thinking that I wish I'd known him better, too."

"We'll find answers," Damien said. Red nodded. Because when a man like Damien Stark made a promise like that ... well, you had to believe him. "There is something I'm curious about."

Red sat up, his head tilted slightly as he studied his friend. "What's that?"

"Anything you need from me or Stark Security, you only have to ask. You know that. But with your skills, I'd think you'd be comfortable handling this on your own. Or with your brother. Working on his own time, of course," Damien added with a grin. Because now Renly was a full-time operative with Stark Security.

"My skills?" Prickles of awareness straightened his spine. "Not sure what you mean. And I'm just one guy."

"Your experience served my wife well when you protected her during that hostage situation. But I wouldn't have expected anything less from a former SWAT officer."

Red heard the question—or maybe it was an accusation—in Damien's voice. "What do you think you know?"

To Damien's credit, he didn't deny. "I know that you never served on a SWAT team, even though that's what you told me after you took that bullet. So why did you say that you did?"

Red shrugged. "Maybe I wanted you to feel secure about who'd been protecting your wife."

"The crisis was already over when you told me. You could have been anyone with the courage to use themself as a shield against a bullet. You chose SWAT. You chose a lie. I want to know why."

Red leaned forward, looking directly into Damien's dual-colored eyes. "I like you. And Renly damn sure respects you. But even a man like you doesn't always get what he wants."

Damien smiled. "You're right. I don't. But I always try. Usually I succeed. I'm stubborn that way. In your case, I wanted to know more about you. Like you said, you saved my wife's life. And I'm always on the lookout for talent."

"I told you I wasn't interested in working for Stark Security."

"And if I'd stopped pushing after the first no in any business negotiation, I wouldn't be where I am today."

Red exhaled. "What is it you think you know?"

"You were the SOC, one of the most secret and elite groups under that umbrella of Special Forces. You have skills. You spent time in Romania. And you left the service after coming home."

Red forced himself not to react. "I'm impressed. How exactly did you find all of that?"

"I told you. I'm tenacious."

Red drew a deep breath, wondering how much Damien knew. The silence lingered, and it became a point of pride not to speak first.

Red won.

"Those must have been interesting missions," Damien said. "I know a bit about human trafficking network operations in Romania. We've dealt with the fallout from a network run by a man named Corbu."

"I know the name. His, and his lieutenants."

"I thought you might."

Once again, silence hung between them. Red looked toward the flagstone path, but only the uniformed officer was there now. Renly and the detective must have gone inside.

"I think you'd be an asset." Damien's voice was level, but Red thought he heard an undertone of compassion. As if Damien understood some of what had gone down.

"I'll think about it." *When hell freezes over.* "In the meantime, just so we're clear, I do intend to handle this myself. It's personal. But I'll likely need op tech and remote assistance, not to mention backup."

"Again, you have it. Whatever you need, no questions asked. And, Red," Damien added, "that's not a one-time offer. Anytime, anywhere. Whatever you need, tomorrow or ten years from now."

"I won't turn it down, but I think you're being overly generous."

"No," Damien said. "I'm not."

Red nodded, thinking of Nikki and the connection between the two of them that was so vibrant it practically lit up a room. "I get it," he said softly, his heart turning over as he saw Jo step into the garden from the tasting room, a uniformed officer at her side.

He realized what he'd said, and almost tried to cover. But he let the words linger. They were true, after all. Maybe that made him the world's biggest asshole, but he loved her. He had for years.

And there wasn't a damn thing he intended to do about that except be the best friend he could possibly be.

He didn't realize that he'd stood until she turned toward him. Even from this distance, he could see her red, swollen eyes.

"Go on," Damien said gently, now also standing. "She's going to need you."

Red didn't answer. Just hurried toward her, and she did the same. They met on the grass between the path and his table, and she threw herself into his arms, then wept as though she'd been keeping it all bottled inside until she saw him.

He held her, hoping his arms around her were

some comfort, though how could they be? She'd just lost her husband. What could possibly erase the pain?

Her body shook, the tremors cutting through him, then slowing as she caught her breath, calmed her shaking, and finally stepped back out of the circle of his arms.

It took all his strength not to draw her back in. He told himself that he needed comfort, too. But it was more than that. He needed *her*. He always had. But oh, God, not like this. Never like this.

"You called," she said, her eyes meeting his. "I tried to text back but I didn't have a signal, and I was going to call you back as soon as I got home. But then the officer was waiting in the driveway and—and—"

"I know. Jo, I know."

Tears flowed, and she clutched his hands, searching his face. "Then it's true? Mel's really dead?"

"I'm so sorry. Yes, it's true."

CHAPTER THREE

Red's words hit me with the force of an anvil. Stupid, I suppose. After all, I'd come home schlepping groceries only to find a police cruiser in my driveway, along with the horrible news that my husband was dead.

I believed them, but at the same time, maybe I hadn't. Maybe I'd just been numb, and Red's words have sent reality crashing down on me.

I hug myself, feeling lost and unsure, my hands holding so tight to Red's I'm probably crushing bone. "I can't wrap my head around it. Suicide? Why would he—"

"Mrs. Swift?"

I turn to see a dark-haired woman in a pantsuit striding toward me, a badge worn like a lanyard around her neck. "I'm Detective Amaro," she says in a voice laced with compassion. "Is there somewhere we could talk?"

I glance sideways at Red, then nod. "Um, yes. Mel's office? But can I—I mean, I need to see him. I need to know—I mean, what if you're wrong?" It's a stupid thing to say. Of course they're not wrong. But I can't truly believe it until I see Mel's body.

His body.

"Certainly," she says kindly. "We'll go there first."

A shiver courses through me, and I reach for Red's hand. "Stay with me?"

His eyes flick briefly to the detective, but she nods, and I'm grateful not to have to go through this alone. My heart hurts and my eyes sting with the tears I've been holding back. I feel numb, but there is anger boiling beneath. Anger and loss and betrayal. *Suicide?*

I want answers. I want to curl up in bed and cry. I want it to go away.

Most of all, I'm glad Red is beside me, because if anyone can get me through this, it's him.

I follow the detective into the distillery to the fermentation room. There's someone in a T-shirt stenciled with *Coroner's Office* zipping my husband into a body bag. The detective leads me there, and I follow with Red behind me. He puts his hand gently on my shoulder when we come to a stop.

"This is Mrs. Swift," Detective Amaro says. "She'd like to see her husband."

"I'm sorry for your loss," the medical guy says, but I barely hear him. I'm too focused on his hand tugging the zipper down, then spreading the black plastic cocoon away so that I can see Mel's face. It's been wiped clean, but there are still bits of the mash in his hair.

I turn away. "Thank you," I whisper. The officer who drove me here told me that he'd died in the fermentation tub, but even so I ask, "How did this happen? You can stand in those tubs. How can someone force themselves to drown?" I turn back to Red. "It doesn't make any sense."

"We believe that he tampered with the carbon dioxide scrubbers," the detective says, "then got into the tub. As he started to lose consciousness, he would have slipped under. I am truly sorry," she adds, and I realize that I've put my hand up to cover my mouth. A tear trickles down my cheek, and I wipe it away, sniffing.

"You *believe*?" I look pointedly up at the security cameras. "Didn't you watch the footage?"

She shakes her head. "It appears he turned them off, as he did with the other safety measures."

I hug myself, still in shock at Mel's death, much less that he'd concocted such an elaborate one.

"Would you like to stay here a bit longer?" The detective's gentle voice catches my attention.

I shake my head and reach for Red, unsure if my legs are strong enough to support me. *Why.* Why would he do this? I know there were things troubling him, but never once did he seem suicidal.

Then again, we weren't really spending that much time together lately.

I barely notice the walk back to Mel's office. I sit on the small sofa, with Red beside me. The detective pulls out one of the guest chairs at Mel's desk and sits as well.

"Because of the note, we are approaching this as a suicide. But at the same time, we need to make further inquiries."

"Of course. Yes. I can't believe he'd do this." Beside me, Red squeezes my hand hard, and I squeeze back, grateful for the support.

"Had he been acting differently recently? Any depression? Trouble at home or at work?"

"I—" I draw in a breath. I don't want to go there, but I know I have to. "I asked him for a divorce."

Beside me, I feel Red shift. I glance that way and see the surprise in his eyes. I'm surprised, too. He and Mel were best friends, but apparently this is news to him.

The detective must also have noticed Red's reaction, because the next question is addressed to him. "You didn't know? Your friend and partner, but he didn't tell you that his wife wanted a divorce?"

"No. This is the first I'm hearing of it."

"We'd grown apart," I say, though no one has asked me to elaborate. "We've been married five years, but the last three..." I trail off with a shake of my head. "It wasn't working," I say simply. "I kept hoping things would get better, but about six months ago, I told him we should separate. He said we should try harder, but nothing changed. Three months ago, I hired an attorney and drew up settlement papers."

"I see. And what stage is the divorce in now?"

I shake my head. "He still hasn't signed. I didn't want to push or formally file with the court. I know him. He's slow to wrap his head around things, but I knew he'd realize I was right. I—I'd hoped we could still be friends, but we couldn't stay married." I tug my hand from Red's and clasp my own together. "We made a mistake getting married in the first place."

The detective nods slowly. "And did you see any change in his behavior in the last three months? In his mood?"

"You mean any signs that he was suicidal?" I shake my head. "God, no. He was distant and hurt, but nothing like that."

"Did he move out? Did you?"

She knows I didn't, obviously, since the officer found me at the house.

"Not technically," I say. "But he stayed away most nights."

"Where?"

"He didn't tell me." I look at Red. "I assumed with you." Red shakes his head, and a spark of anger rises in me. "Well, there you go. Another reason I was right to file."

Red and the detective exchange glances, and I exhale, frustrated and angry. Angry with Mel for killing himself. Angry with myself for feeling like it's my fault. And angry with the woman I am almost certain he'd been fucking behind my back, but he'd been too ball-less to admit as much even when it was clear the marriage was over.

"Another reason?" The detective was looking at me, compassion in her eyes. "Was your husband having an affair?"

"Yes. No." I shake my head. "The truth is, I don't know. But I think so. He has a friend—well, a new friend—who owns a hotel. And for about the last six months he'd stay there overnight sometimes. He'd text and tell me he'd drunk too much and that his friend comped him a room."

"A hotel?" Red asks. "Which friend?"

"Just a guy he met in some CrossFit group. I don't remember his name. But if it's important, I can find out. I remember that this guy needed some corporate legal work done, and Mel referred him to one of the partners. I'm a legal assistant," I add, though the detective probably already knows that.

"Did he end up working with your firm?"

"I don't know. I work on the litigation side. Is it important?" I can't imagine why it would be.

"Probably not," she says, confirming my thoughts. "We'll let you know if we need to pursue that. But I don't think we will. I am sorry, Mrs. Swift. Dealing with suicide is hard enough without the invasive questions."

"No, it's okay. I want answers, too."

"Was this the guy he was talking with about the supply contract?" Red asks.

"I don't know. He never mentioned a supply contract to me. Which doesn't mean anything. It's been a minute since he talked to me about important stuff. But to be honest, I don't think he was negotiating anything. I think—" I cut myself off. "Never mind."

"Ms. Swift. Please."

I don't want to talk about it, but I know I have to. "I think that was bullshit to cover the affair, okay? He told me that if I didn't want him at home, he'd stay in a room at the hotel, but he wasn't going to tell me where. He said if I couldn't stand not knowing where he was or what he was doing, then I must not really want a divorce, and I couldn't have it both ways. He didn't say so, but I assume he'd been using the room as a place to take his lover. Now, I don't know. Maybe there was no hotel at all, and he was just going to her place."

I swallow. "And the truth is, he was right. I didn't care."

Red puts a hand on my shoulder, and I draw a breath, letting his strength and compassion calm me. What I want is to scoot closer so I can put my head on his shoulder and cry, knowing he'll comfort me. But I can't do that now, not while this detective is asking her questions. And I shouldn't do it later. Because with Red, there's the danger of compassion turning to something more.

Or, more honestly, the danger is that I'd want it to.

I shift, subtly dislodging his touch.

The detective is watching me. "You seem to care now."

I nod. "It was ... frustrating ... that he wouldn't agree to the divorce. That he kept blowing off signing the papers. And it pissed me off that he was stalling while he was sleeping with someone else. Who does that?"

I hate that my anger is so close to the surface, especially now with my emotions all confused and tangled. Anger, sadness, confusion, betrayal. I don't know what to think or feel. And apparently I'm just going to feel everything, and all at the same time, and hope I don't sound like this is all about me.

Because no matter how angry he made me, Mel is dead, and he didn't deserve that.

I draw a breath, trying to rein in my emotions. "The bottom line is that we'd drifted apart, Detective. Couples do. But—but I still love him, just not like that. And I don't understand why he'd—"

I can't talk anymore through the tears clogging my throat. I wipe my eyes and my nose. Whatever dam I'd put up to hold back the waterworks has broken, and I bend over sobbing, my shoulders shaking as Red gently rubs my back.

"It's possible he saw this lover as an escape route," Detective Amaro says. "If she wasn't interested in more than that, he may have felt disconnected. Unrooted. Depending on his mental state, that could have led him to believe he had no other option. I've seen this before."

I nod; what she says makes sense, even if I hate every word of it. After a moment, I run my hand under my nose. "Wasn't Jessn here? He would have been on shift, right?" I look to Red.

He shakes his head. "Mel told him to go home."

"But— I—" I close my mouth, unsure what I even want to say. "This is surreal."

"You're doing fine," Red says, squeezing my hand.

"Were there other things that made you believe he was having an affair?"

I swallow, feeling the walls closing in around

me. Was this never going to end? "I—yes. Little things. But Detective, I already feel shitty enough that he killed himself. And I—it's just that if he killed himself because he was upset about the divorce or his mistress blowing him off, there's nothing I can do but feel horrible about that. And nothing personal, but right now, I just want to go home and cry. It's not like we can ever really know why he did it, so haven't I told you enough?"

"Unless you think this wasn't a suicide," Red adds, "in which case, Ms. Swift has the right to counsel before you question her."

I gape at him. Does he actually think the cops believe I had something to do with Mel's death?

"As I told your brother, we see nothing to suggest it wasn't suicide. But we do like the fullest picture possible in our report."

I draw in a breath and gird myself to dive into our emotional baggage. Red's hand on my arm stops me.

"She's told you plenty, and you can always ask more later. Right now, she needs time to grieve."

For a moment, the detective says nothing. Then she inclines her head. "Of course." Her eyes are warm and her expression genuine when she meets my eyes. "I truly am sorry."

And with that, she heads out the door, leaving Red and me alone in Mel's office.

"I can't believe this is happening," I say. I

manage a smile that is probably more like a grimace. "You should have been a lawyer instead of a distiller."

His gaze never wavers as he meets my eyes and says, "There are a lot of should haves in my life."

I swallow and look at the floor, unable to shake the feeling that he's talking about me. Worse, unable to avoid the horrible, guilty truth that I want him to be.

"I—Red, listen. I'm so glad you're here, and that I don't have to go through this alone. It was the three of us for so long. But—well, do you mind? I just need to be alone for a bit."

"I get it." He stands, then helps me to my feet before pulling me close for a hug. "We'll get through this."

I nod. We will. We have to.

"We should talk, though," he adds, his voice lowering. "But not here. Tonight?"

I shake my head. "Not tonight. I know we need to talk. I mean, I guess I'm now the only Swift in Swift Red Distillery, right? But I can't deal with any of that today. I just want to go home, put on a sad movie, and cry myself to sleep."

"Jo..."

"Tomorrow?"

I think he's going to argue, but then he nods. "Nine o'clock. I'll come over. I'll make you breakfast."

"So you'll pour cereal into a bowl?"

He almost grins. "I didn't say it would be a good breakfast."

"Thanks," I whisper, for both offering to feed me and adding a bit of levity to the moment. I rise up and kiss his cheek, breathing in the familiar scent of sandalwood. I don't really want him to go. I feel fragile. Unanchored. But even though I've lost my husband, I don't feel alone. I have Red to thank for that.

"See you tomorrow," he says, pulling away from me, then heading out of what has now become my office.

The door closes with a *snick*, the soft sound remarkably final. I draw in a deep breath and tell myself I'm not going to cry.

Then I go around the desk and sit in Mel's chair. I pull open the middle drawer, and there it is —the thin sheath of blue-back papers. The kind I see every day in my job.

I flip to the last page and confirm what I already know.

He didn't sign the divorce papers before he died.

I really am a widow.

And there, at my late husband's desk, I finally break down and sob.

CHAPTER FOUR

Hours passed, but finally Renly and Red were alone in the distillery. Jo was the first to leave, having gone home after the cops dismissed her. Since she'd arrived in a police cruiser, Damien had offered to drive her home, but when Red remembered that Mel's new Lexus was parked in one of the employee slots, she decided to drive herself.

Damien left soon after, reiterating his offer of whatever help Red or the distillery needed. Red had promised to take him up on that. He meant it, too. Damien Stark had resources, and Red was willing to call in any favors he could to find the bastard who'd killed his partner.

Once the cops and the personnel from the Coroner's Office had cleared out, Renly offered to close up. "I've done it before. And you've had a hell of a day."

Red almost laughed; wasn't that the truth? But ultimately, he shook his head. "I called in Jessn and Charlie G. They're both on their way over. They'll get the system checks running, drain and sterilize that bin, and clean up in the fermentation room."

He said the last with a shudder. He'd told his seconds-in-command that he'd do that himself. It wasn't as if there was much of a mess. After all, the coroner's office had taken the body.

But they'd both insisted that Red go home, assuring him that they'd take care of it.

"Good," Renly said. "They'll know what to do."

"They will. In the mean time, I need to report the whole incident to the health department."

"What's the process?"

Red chuckled. "No clue." Murder in the fermentation room hadn't been something he'd added to his checklist when they'd originally got the business underway. "Hopefully we'll be permitted to keep the other tubs going, but we need a clean bill of health on the distillery as soon as possible."

"You need to get out in front of the press, too."

"Already thought of that. I texted our PR company. They'll manage the messaging, and I'm going to insist we close the tasting room to the public for a week and operate the distillery on a skeleton staff out of respect for Mel."

What he didn't say aloud was that he needed that week to find the MacGuffin, then use it as bait to take out Mel's killer.

"Is a week enough?" Renly asked, making clear that he understood Red's unspoken meaning.

"I think so." He damn sure hoped so. He ran his fingers through his hair, hating the fact that he had to think about such things instead of simply mourning his friend. Things having to do with both the business of the distillery and the business of revenge.

Because he *was* going to avenge his friend, no matter how much he dreaded skirting that dark world of criminals and torture and death.

He drew in a breath as he crossed his arms, holding onto his opposite forearms. His palms closed over the five-inch long scars that marred both arms, and he drew in a breath, the feel of the mutilated flesh as potent as a talisman.

Well, wasn't it?

His body stiffened as he fought off the rising memories. He didn't want to go back into that world, but he had no choice. He couldn't turn his back on his friend any more than he could have stayed away from Nikki Stark that night in New York.

And he damn sure couldn't push this off on

someone else. Not Renly. Not Stark Security. Not when the bastards had threatened Jo.

Hell, even if they hadn't threatened her. This was *his* distillery, Mel had been his partner, and Jo deserved answers.

"I can wait with you until Jessn and Charlie G get here," Renly said, those all-too-knowing eyes studying his face.

"I appreciate it, bro. But I should probably be alone to tell them what's up. I only said there was a crisis, and that I needed them to get here as soon as possible. Suicide's a hard subject. I don't want them to feel uncomfortable reacting around you."

"I still can't believe he did that," Renly said, making clear he understood the need not to talk about the murder. "Killing himself, I mean. I never would have expected it of Mel."

"I know. The whole thing blows my mind. But he really had been acting strange lately." That part was not a lie. He'd been moody and evasive. And from what Jo had told him, it wasn't just at work.

"Why do you think he did it?" Renly asked.

Red translated the question as *what is this thing that they're supposedly looking for?*

"I don't know."

"Do you think you'll ever figure it out? Do you think Jo understands what he was going through?"

"I doubt it," Red said. "Whatever was going on with him, I think he held it close to the vest."

"You should go see her."

Red agreed wholeheartedly. "She wanted to be alone tonight. I considered going by and talking to her, anyway, but decided that sleep probably is the right thing." That decision to let Jo go the night thinking it was suicide had been a hard one.

Renly's voice was sympathetic when he said, "In a situation like this, nothing's ever easy. She'll be better prepared to deal with this in the morning."

Some of the tension drained from him, knowing that Renly thought he made the right call, too. "Come on," he said. "I'll walk you to your car."

"Sure." Renly said, his expression curious as they moved through the property to the customer parking area.

They paused by Renly's Ducati, a damn sweet bike that Red openly envied.

"Aren't you the gentleman?" Renly's mouth curved with mirth.

"Nah. I just wanted to look at that bike of yours. You know, you can always park in an employee spot. Though I'm glad you didn't. Let's me know you know your place."

"Yeah, I'm smart that way."

"Listen, there's one more thing." He chose his words carefully. He'd moved their conversation to the parking lot because the odds of surveillance on the customers was slim, but he had no way to be sure. For all he knew there was one video-only camera in the fermentation room. On the other hand, the whole place could be wired for sound and video.

And that was the one thing he did want Renly and Stark Security to jump on. "I'm glad you came —God knows I needed the moral support. But I didn't just call about that. The truth is if we'd had a better system, we might have caught this before Mel was able to kill himself. An alarm when he shut some of the safety protocols off. I don't know. Something."

"You want to upgrade your system."

"That's the kind of thing your company can do, right?" By which, of course, he meant Stark Security.

"Absolutely."

They shared a smile. They both knew that while it was in fact among the things that Stark Security did, it occupied a tiny percentage of the workflow. In reality, Stark Security did so much more, but the deeper level things were through referral only. Things the general public didn't know. Things that only a very few select groups and individuals understood as the depth of the agency's expertise.

"Can you get me a quote? We have a base level, but I want the gold standard. Where anything that's changed is logged. And if there's anything even remotely unusual, I personally get a text."

What he didn't say was that while all that was true, he also wanted a sweep of the entire building to locate and get rid of any bugs or recording devices that whoever killed Mel had installed anywhere on the property.

From the way Renly was nodding slowly, Red was certain his brother understood. "If it's okay by you, I can bring the tech guys in tonight and we can probably have something spec'd out for you in the next day or so."

"Perfect," Red said as Renly mounted the bike, then slipped on his helmet.

"Give Abby a kiss for me, and tell her thanks for the virtual hugs," Red said. Renly had texted to tell her what was going on, and she'd sent Red her condolences, promising to call him soon. He'd expected nothing less, of course. She might be Renly's fiancée, but she'd been one of Red's best friends since junior high. Abby knew Mel, too, of course, but they'd only met after Renly and Abby had reconnected in LA. Reconnected in every sense of the word, he added, smiling to himself.

Renly sat up a bit straighter, as if just the mention of Abby took some weight off his shoulders. "The day I've had, you can bet she's going to be getting lots of kisses. I'm holding that woman close."

Red nodded, trying to ignore the small, hollow place in his stomach. He knew he could never have what Renly and Abby had. He knew he couldn't be that guy. But oh, how he envied his brother.

"And you're absolutely certain you don't want me to stay?"

"Positive," Red assured him. "The guys will be here soon, then I'll go home."

"Promise me you'll get some rest. This will all be here in the morning."

Translation, Red needed to be able to think straight to figure out what the fuck was going on. "Agreed. I'll touch base tomorrow."

Renly started the bike, then turned onto Santa Monica Boulevard right as Jessn pulled in. Red crossed to where his manager was parking, then pulled him into a hug when he exited the car.

"I can't believe this," Jessn said. It's so fucked up. I never would have thought Mel would off himself." He drew a breath, then studied Red. "You okay, boss?"

"Been better."

"Charlie G's about an hour behind me, but you don't need to wait. I'll take care of the place. You just go take care of you."

He dragged his fingers through his hair. "Yeah. Yeah, I'm gonna do that. Listen, the cameras are back online, and most of the gauges. You'll need to make hourly rounds, but I think you should actually do them by the half hour. You okay with that?"

"I'm not afraid of ghosts, if that's what you mean. And Mel wouldn't hurt me anyway."

"No, he wouldn't." And no one else had reason to. Not if they wanted Red to cooperate in finding the missing package.

He followed Jessn into the tasting room, then gave him the rest of the rundown. "I got it, Red. Seriously. Charlie G and I've got your back."

"I know you do," he said. "I'm going to get some stuff out of my office, and then head out. I'll lock up behind me."

"You got it."

Red watched, as Jessn left the tasting room, crossed through the garden area, and entered the distillery. Then, like a man sleepwalking, he headed to the bar. He pulled out a glass, took one of the open bottles of whiskey, and poured a shot. He stared at the glass, then reached for it slowly.

"*Fuck.*" He snatched up the glass, then tossed the contents into the sink. *Not like this. Not for this reason.*

With the weight of the day heavy on his shoulders, he headed out the front door, locking it behind him. Customer parking was in front, but the employee section was in back, and he walked to the side of the building. It was getting late; the sun had set about half an hour ago, and the world seemed to exist only in shades of gray.

He shivered, then told himself to get over it. He wasn't a superstitious man. And any ghosts that might be around would be more inclined to help him than to hurt him.

He headed to his car, a Toyota hybrid he'd bought a few years ago. He got out his key fob as he walked, heard the sharp beep as the doors unlocked, and took another step toward the vehicle.

Then the pain hit him. Full-body pain, like fire ants coursing over his body and through his blood, only a million times worse. He lost all control, his muscles no longer obeying, and he shook and shook right down to his core.

Taser.

His mind and body were too fried to form any more coherent thoughts, but he knew what this was. Had experienced it in training, and that had been more than enough. He wanted to turn, to see who'd done this to him, but he had no control. Hell, he could barely think, and soon enough his legs turned to liquid and he collapsed on the ground, unable to do anything except bear the pain from the two points that had shot out from the weapon and made contact.

And then, just as fast as it came, the pain was gone. He sat up breathing hard, his knife already in his hand as he searched for whoever could have been his attacker. But there was no one.

His phone pinged and he reached for it. Only his screen was dark. No call, no text.

Mel's phone. He reached for it and saw the text on the lock screen:

You are not safe.
The people you care about aren't safe.
Not until you tell us what we want to know.
Where is the package that Swift stole?

He texted back: *I told you I don't know.*

Then I suggest you find out. In the meantime,
perhaps we'll ask someone else who might know.
Don't try to trace this number. It's dead as of now.
We'll be in touch.

His brain was still slow, and it took a minute for him to process the message, but as soon as he did, he forced himself to his feet and yanked open the car door.

Jo. The fuckers were going after Jo!

CHAPTER FIVE

I drive home on autopilot, following the route from Hollywood to our cottage-like house in Studio City. I don't know what to think or even what I *am* thinking. I'm just driving, lost in a storm of dark emotions, confusion, and guilt.

I know it's not my fault that my husband killed himself. I know there must have been deeper issues going on. But surely I should have picked up on something? Had we really drifted so far apart that I had absolutely no clue how far into the dark my husband had slipped?

Yes, I think. *Yes, yes, yes.*

Tears prick my eyes, and I blink, trying to clear my vision.

I know I shouldn't blame myself, but how can I not? He was my husband, and no matter how distant we'd become, I still loved him.

How could I have been so blind?

It's a refrain that plays through my head over and over and over as I move past the familiar landmarks and finally pull into our driveway and park next to my Fiat.

I've never liked Mel's new car, and I don't understand why he wanted to buy it. He'd never been one for status symbols, at least I hadn't thought so. But he'd snatched this up like a security blanket. Now, ironically, it's my security blanket, because I don't want to get out. In this car, I'm in a cozy little bubble where I can pretend that everything is okay and the world can't touch me. But I know I can't stay. I have to get out.

I have to face all of the guilt that goes along with losing a husband I wanted to divorce.

"You can do this," I say, and even though I'm not at all sure that I'm right about that, I push open the door and make my way into the house. It's small and clean and smells of vanilla, and despite the memories that I know will soon assault me, the simple act of stepping inside makes me feel more centered.

Sure, there were tears and arguments as I begged him to just sign the papers so we could both get on with our lives without having involve a judge.

But there were good times, too. Laughter and sweet memories that I will always cherish.

"Mel," I whisper. "Why the hell didn't you just talk to me? Did you think I wasn't your friend anymore? That I didn't love you? I still did—I still do. Just not the way you wanted me to."

There's no reply, of course. And considering I'm certain he was sleeping with someone else, maybe he no longer loved me. Maybe he got lost in his guilt about the affair.

So many maybes. And an utter dearth of answers.

I'm about to head into the kitchen for a glass of bourbon when there's a sharp knock on the door. I shift directions, almost stumbling over Rambo, our fat and lazy cat, who's magically appeared between my legs from wherever he'd been hiding.

He rubs my legs as I peer through the peephole. I recognize Abby's bouncy curls and wide eyes immediately, and I pull open the door, then find myself engulfed in her hug.

"Renly called me earlier," she says. "He said that Red had just told him that Mel was dead and he was on his way to the distillery. I was in Burbank, so I came here to check on you, but I didn't see your car. So I thought I'd try one more time before heading home."

"I'm so glad you did." I usher her in, and we head to the sofa in the living area.

"Was it an accident? Renly didn't know what happened, and I haven't talked to him since. He left one voicemail, but all it said was that he'd tell me later when he saw me."

I start to tell her that it was suicide. Instead, I burst into tears.

"Oh, Jo, it'll be okay."

She gets up immediately and goes into the kitchen, then pours two glasses of whiskey. It was one of the smarter moves in my life to marry a man who wanted to open a distillery, especially as I've always preferred whiskey to wine. She brings them over, hands me one of the glasses, then reaches out as if to toast. "To Mel and the memories," she says.

I nod, and though it's simple, the toast seems completely appropriate.

She settles on the sofa beside me, then reaches for my hand. I take it eagerly, grateful for the comfort.

We haven't known each other that long in the grand scheme of things. We met at a party at the distillery right about the time Renly asked her to marry him. It's been less than a year, but Abby and I hit it off, and she's become one of my closest friends.

"Do you want to talk about it?" she asks.

I shake my head. "I really don't. Right now, I'm trying to forget. I know I can't—but just for a little while, can we pretend everything is normal?"

"Are you kidding? Of course. Whatever you

need. Is it okay that I'm here? Would you rather be alone?"

"No, it's great. But aren't you in the middle of some big upgrade?" Abby's a partner in a software development company with Nikki Stark, and it seems like they're always in the middle of rolling out a new product or an upgrade.

"Nope. I'm golden. We got that finished over the weekend."

Reality smacks me in the head. "I can't believe I said that. Of course you're taking the week off. And I'm really looking forward to the party."

She practically glows, and I wonder if I looked like that in the days before I married Mel. Honestly, I don't think so.

"The timing's now kind of terrible," she says.

"No," I say. "Everyone will want to have a chance to celebrate. Take our minds off things." Abby and Renly are getting married on Friday in front of a judge, but immediately after, Damien Stark is throwing them a party at his Malibu home. They'll stay in his guesthouse that night, then head off to a honeymoon in Italy.

"My mother thinks I'm crazy not to want a big wedding, but that's not us. I want to get married intimately, then have a celebration."

"I totally applaud you. And I'm really happy for you both." I mean it, too. Abby and Renly have been lifelong friends, and you can see their connection crackle around them. Honestly, it makes me a little jealous. Because that's not something Mel and I ever had.

"Thanks. But I didn't mean to hijack the conversation. You must be in shock." As I nod, she continues. "Was there some sort of accident at the distillery, or—"

"He killed himself," I blurt, shocking us both. And then, suddenly, all those damn tears are back. "I'm sorry. I didn't—"

"Don't you dare finish that sentence," she says. "Jo, my God." She puts her arms around me, and I let her pull me close. "I had no idea."

"He didn't even leave a note. No explanation. Just *sorry*."

"Do you want me to stay the night? Renly will understand, and we can hang out and get drunk and watch movies. I mean, it sounds as reasonable a plan as any, don't you think?"

I laugh despite myself. "It sounds like an amazing plan, but all I want is to finish this whiskey and go to bed. What's that saying? Even if tomorrow isn't a better day at least it's a different one?"

Abby rolls her eyes. "That's not the way the saying goes, and tomorrow *will* be a better day."

"Honestly, I think by default it has to be. The only way to go is up."

"Cheers to that," she says, and we clink glasses.

"Can you hang out for a little bit? Maybe watch some mindless television?"

"Of course. I can," Abby says, and I turn on the television. I scroll through the streaming services until we come across *The IT Crowd*, and she squeals for me to stop. "It's a hoot," she promises, when I tell her I've never heard of it. And she's right. It's not only funny, but it's clear why she loves it, what with working with computers herself.

"It's great," I tell her after we finish the third episode. "But I think I'm televisioned out."

"Do you want me to go? Or I can stay and make you some food. Distract you. I can stay the whole night if you need me to. Truly."

I shake my head. "No. Seriously. I'm fine. It means a lot that you came over. Tell Renly that I'm glad he was there today. I know that Red must be losing his mind. He was more married to Mel than I was, when you think about it."

"There are all sorts of partnerships. And all sorts of friendships."

I'd been thinking that very thing. Because Mel and Red and I had been like a perfect trifecta during college. And back in those days I'd been absolutely certain how it would work out for all of us. Funny how things never seem to go as you planned them.

She reaches down and scratches Rambo's ears. He'd disappeared when she came in, but now that he's decided that Abby—who he knows well—won't be attacking him anytime soon, he's decided to emerge.

"Hey there, Rambo." When she bends over and picks him up, the cat immediately goes boneless, hanging completely limp until she deposits him in her lap. "Just a quick scratch behind the ears, then I have to go."

"You embarrass him every time you do that. He supposed to be the big, tough warrior of the house. You pet and stroke him like he's a little baby."

She bends down and nuzzles her nose against his fluffy cat forehead. "He's my wittle snooker-wookums," she says in a baby voice, making me laugh. She tilts her head sideways and grins at me. "I guess my work here is done. This one will look after you the rest of the night?"

"I promise you, he is very good at helping take my mind off things."

"Promise to call me if you need anything."

"Swear," I say, then carry the cat as we walked to the door. I see Abby out, but ignore Rambo's chomping at the bit to do the same. We do let him outside on occasion, but only in the backyard. We have a fence made of corrugated steel that matches the distillery, and it's impossible for a cat to climb. He goes out, sleeps on the concrete patio, and then comes inside feeling like he's made his rounds and is protecting home and hearth.

Now though, he's staying inside for his dinner.
I close the front door and follow him into the
kitchen.

He knows the routine as well as I do.

"I'm sorry to tell you, baby kitty, but your
daddy won't be coming back."

I realize tears are trickling down my cheeks as I
put his cat food on a platter. I don't know how to
handle this frustration. This anger at knowing that
there was something going on with Mel. That if
he'd just talked to me, maybe I could've helped
him. At least steered him toward therapy.

Because there *was* something going on, just like
I thought. Maybe not an affair, though. He didn't
have a history of depression, but maybe something
happened that he never told me about. Or maybe it
really was an affair, and he got his heart broken and
felt trapped with me.

Bottom line? I don't know. And the not
knowing is killing me.

I look down at Rambo. Sometimes, I think it
really would be nice to be a cat.

With a sigh, I pour myself a little bit more
whiskey, just because it will help me sleep. I head
toward the back door, calling for the cat. "If you
want to do outside time today, now's your chance.
I'm going to bed early, and you're going to be stuck
inside if you don't do it now. I'll give you fifteen
minutes and then you're coming back in."

As if he understands every word I said, he trots over to the door. I let him out, close only the screen door so that I can hear if he howls at something, then set the timer that sits on the table by the back door. He uses that time to sniff the flowers, chase the birds, and sprawl on the concrete, still warm from the day.

While he's in kitty heaven, I eat ice cream. It's not my usual dinner, but today I need it. Heaps of vanilla with chocolate sauce drizzled all over it.

I'm licking the spoon when the timer goes off, and glance over to see that he's already standing at the screen.

Who says you can't train a cat?

He meows, lower and more growly than his usual voice, and I wonder if this isn't one of those evenings where he can sense the dog next door.

"What's up, buddy?" I ask as I push open the screen. I expect him to saunter over the threshold as always. Instead, Rambo hisses, then races inside the house, brushing my legs and actually making me stumble.

I turn, watching him run. "What are you—"

My words turn into a gasp as someone grabs my wrist and yanks me outside, then slams me back into the side of the house. My attacker is dressed all in black from head to toe, and he has a knife pressed against my throat.

My heart is pounding so hard I can barely hear my thoughts much less what my attacker is saying.

"Where are they?" he says in a voice low and gravelly. "Where is the package your husband took from us?"

I shake my head. "I don't know what you're talking about." About six-two, I think. Raspy voice. Brown eyes.

"Don't lie."

"I'm not. I swear." I hear the tremor in my voice. "I have no idea what you mean."

"You damn well better find out, bitch." He takes the knife, and before I even realize what's happening, he flicks my upper lip. The blade is so sharp I barely feel it, but I can immediately taste the blood, and go rigid with fear.

"Please, I—"

He flips me around and tosses me back inside. I stumble to my knees, and by the time I've righted myself, he's gone.

I take five quick, deep breaths, then scramble for the back door. I close it, then lock it, then simply stand there, my body numb with a combination of fear and relief. I want to go outside and see how he got into the yard. He must have used bolt cutters on the gate's padlock. Or used a ladder to get over the steel fencing. But there's no way I'm going outside right now.

I take another deep breath, then go into my

bedroom and get the handgun I keep there. My ex-military father started taking me to the range when I was ten years old. He taught me gun safety and how to shoot straight. But, dammit, you never seem to have a gun on your person when you need one.

I have it now, though fat lot of good it'll do me since the attacker is thankfully gone.

Then—holy shit—there's a rattle at the front door.

The son of a bitch is back? Rage bubbles through me, overtaking the rising fear, and I rush forward. I rip open the door and level the gun right at his face. "No way, you fucker."

"Jesus Christ, Jo, it's me."

Red is standing in front of me with his hands up in the air. At least that's what my brain registers in that moment. But somehow he's moved, because a half-second later, his hands are no longer in the air, they're around me, and the gun is in his hand.

"If I could do that, so could whoever the hell you meant to be pointing that thing at." His voice is hard, and I can hear both anger and concern.

"I thought you were a bad guy."

"Then why the fuck didn't you run out the back?"

I start to sob. I don't know. I should have. I know that. My father always said the gun was a last resort. But my husband's dead, and I don't know why, and a stranger attacked me, wanting something that Mel had. I have no idea what's going on, and I don't like it. Worst of all, I'm scared.

But I don't say anything or any of that to Red. Instead, I simply look into his eyes, then choke on tears as I say, "I'm having a really bad day."

CHAPTER SIX

"You're bleeding," Red says. His finger brushes my upper lip, and I shiver, turning my face away, embarrassed by how much I want to lean into him. To let him comfort me and wash away my fears.

"It's just a scratch. I'll be okay." I sniffle. The truth is, all I really want to do is curl up and cry and pretend like none of this is happening.

Instead, I tilt my head back, searching his face through the blur of tears. "I'm sorry. I'm sorry I almost shot you, and I'm sorry I'm a mess. I just have no idea what's going on."

"Come on." His voice is as gentle as the palm he presses against my back. "Let's get you settled."

He shuts the door and leads me to the couch, then sits me down. I curl my legs up under me in the corner, then pull a pillow into my lap. He's sitting sideways, facing me, and when he bends forward, for one strange moment, I think he's going to kiss me.

Stranger still, I think I want him to, if only so that I can slip outside of myself, and for a few glorious, blissful moments, forget the hell that has become my world.

But he's not kissing me. Instead, he's looking at my lip. He pulls a tissue from the box on the table and dabs gently at it. I bite my lower lip, but the reaction isn't because of pain. It's because of him—this broad-shouldered man who had once been the focus of my fantasies. A soldier who has seen wounds much worse than mine, now treating me so gently.

A man who, because of grief or loss or lingering terror, has slid quite inappropriately into my thoughts.

I turn away, afraid he can read the truth in my eyes. "It's fine."

"It will be," he agrees. "It's barely a scratch. But facial wounds always bleed a lot. Does it hurt?"

I shake my head, then realize I'm crying, as if in contrast to my negative response. "No. No it doesn't hurt. I just ... God, Red. I'm a mess." I draw in a shuddering breath. "I don't understand what's going on."

"I know." He puts down the tissue and leans forward, taking my hands. "Let's take this one step at a time."

I swallow and nod.

"Tell me what happened before I came. How did you cut your lip? Was someone here? Is that why you got the gun?"

I can tell from his tone that he already knows—or at least suspects—the answer.

"There—there was a man..."

I'm mortified to realize my throat is thick with tears, some of which are now streaming down my cheeks. I pull one hand free and wipe my eyes. "I'm sorry. My emotions are all over the place."

"Of course they are." His voice is as soft as a caress. "It's okay, Jo. Whoever was here is gone now."

I shiver. "I don't understand what's happening."

"I think I do. Part of it, anyway. I'll tell you everything. But I need you to go first. Can you do that for me?"

His voice is soft but steady, as if he's explaining something important to a child. The tone irritates me—not because he's talking down to me, but because I'm actually melting down.

Get it together, girl.

"Yes," I say firmly. "I can do that." I draw a deep breath, then begin. "I have no idea why, but some guy jumped me when I was letting Rambo in." I pull my hands free from Red's, needing to hug myself. "I—I didn't see much. He was all in black."

"He?"

I nod. "I think so. At least that's what his voice sounded like. I'd be surprised if it was a woman."

"So he talked to you, what did he say?"

"It was about Mel—something about Mel having something. He said, 'Where are they,' and then he said he wanted the package Mel took."

As I speak, a horrible thought comes to me, and I'm about to share it with Red. But he speaks first.

"They? You're sure he said *they*?"

I think back, then nod, chills creeping up my spine. "Yes, yes. I'm sure. But Red," I say, hurrying on. "I just realized — I mean, what if it wasn't suicide? Maybe somebody murdered Mel to get this thing."

Red looks at me for so long, I begin to think I'd tossed out the most ridiculous theory ever. Then his face seems to crumple, and I see tears in his eyes.

"You're right," he says, his voice thick. "They murdered him, but he never told them where it is. The murder must have been a mistake," he adds, his voice soft, as if he's working through something. "Kill him, the thing is lost. Unless you or I know where it is."

He's looking at me now, but I can only shake

my head, completely confused. "You're saying you think I'm right? Then we should call the police. They need—"

"No." He grabs my wrist, preventing me from reaching for my phone.

I try to tug my hand back, but he holds on tight. "Red, you're scaring me."

"You can't tell the cops it was murder."

"Why?" My head is spinning, and I'm not sure if it's because this entire conversation is confusing or if I'm overwhelmed by the events of the day.

"Because the killers told me not to."

"They attacked you?"

"No—well, yes. But this was before that. They made it clear that the cops need to keep believing this was suicide."

"Oh." I swallow as that settles in. "Oh," I repeat, then hug myself as icy fear cuts through me. "I think you need to start at the beginning."

He does, telling me how Mel asked to meet him, but didn't show up. At least, that was what Red believed until he found my husband's body in the mash.

"And they called you?"

"Yes. But on Mel's phone. And they showed me—"

He stops, as if he isn't sure he should continue.

"What?"

"Jo, I don't think you should—"

I press two fingers over his lips and shake my head. "No. No way are you playing macho protector guy. I mean, yeah, protect me all you want—I am completely fine with that—but you don't get to dole out the information. He was my husband. I was attacked, too, and for better or worse, I'm your partner in the distillery now." Technically, I always have been since I got my third of the business when I used my savings to help finance the place. But I never participated and only voted if Mel and Red disagreed, which they never did. Now, though, it's just me and Red.

"I mean it," I say. "Whatever it is, I can take it. Don't coddle me."

He runs his fingers through his thick, wavy hair, making it stand up a bit, augmenting the illusion of flames.

"Fine." He swallows as he types in the passcode, then hands me Mel's phone. "But you asked. Go to the last video."

I pause, holding the phone. "You have his passcode?"

The knowledge is like a little twinge to my heart. When we were first married, Mel and I used the same code for computers and phones. Then he changed his, a fact I discovered when I wanted to look back for some photos we'd taken on a trip to

Catalina Island. He emailed me the pictures, but stalled on the passcode. Eventually, I stopped worrying about it. By that time, passcodes were the least of our problems.

"I didn't. They gave it to me. Whoever they are."

I shiver, once again thinking about the affair I'd assumed had been going on. Maybe I was right. Maybe he'd been seduced by some bitch who was using him for some reason.

None of which matters at the moment. The phone has re-locked, so I type in the code Red gives me, then watch, feeling sicker and sicker as a masked stranger tortures my husband, then leaves him to die in a tub of mash.

Numb, I pass the phone back to Red. "I— I— Oh, God."

I clap my hand over my mouth and race to the bathroom. I throw up bile and whiskey, then close the lid and rest my forehead on the cool porcelain. I don't even realize that I'm crying until Red finds me there. He brushes my hair back away from my face, then helps me to my feet.

"I know," he says. "But you need to be strong. We both do."

I nod. I know he's right. Whoever killed Mel has their eyes on me now. Red, too. "What are we supposed to do? I don't know anything about this package. Do you?"

He shakes his head. "Nothing. Or, nothing until a few moments ago. You provided one piece of the puzzle."

"Me? How? I don't know a thing."

"No, but they do. And they let something slip." He's looking at me, as if waiting for me to see this massive clue. But I don't see a thing. "*They*. You told me your attacker said *Where are they*."

"Right, but what—*oh*." I nod, proud of myself for having caught up a bit. "It's one package, but it has multiple things in it. But what? Counterfeit bills? Gems? Blackmail photos?" My love of thriller novels is clearly showing. "And does it matter?"

"It might. Right now, I'm operating on the assumption that any fact we can unearth matters."

I hoist myself up, but my legs still feel wobbly, so I move to sit back down. I'm aiming for the toilet lid and instead end up on the floor, my back against the sink cabinets.

Red had been squatting beside me. Now he moves to the edge of the tub across from me. "They seem to think we know something about the package. Possibly, they're desperate and grasping at straws hoping that Mel told one of us something. But it's also possible that they're positive one or both of us *does* know something."

"Do you?" I ask.

"Not that I know of."

"Same. And it's not as if Mel and I were talking

a lot lately. And God knows there wasn't pillow talk. Not for years."

As soon as the words are out of my mouth, I want to kick myself. Red is the last person with whom I want to discuss my utter lack of a sex life. Especially right now.

"It's possible one of us knows something, but we're not aware that it's relevant."

"For all intents and purposes, that's the same as not knowing."

"Can't argue with that." He grins, and for a moment, it feels as if we're having a normal conversation. "But tell me about the last few months with Mel. Maybe I'll pick up on something you haven't."

"I wish there was more to tell. We hadn't even been talking much. And like I said, he lived here on paper only."

"You wanted a divorce because he'd become distant?"

I shake my head. "No. Well, yes. It started years ago, really. Long before this."

"We don't know what *this* is. Much less when it started."

I swallow, realizing that he's right. "Fair enough. Originally, it was—oh, hell. I think originally it was me. I love Mel—I do. Did. I—" I have to take a breath and pull myself together. "I guess I realized pretty early on that we shouldn't have gotten married in the first place. It was a lot of little things. I tried to make it work, but I guess he felt it, too, because we grew apart. It was such a mess, you know, because we'd been great friends in college, and then..."

I trail off, my voice shaky. I hate spilling all of this onto Red. On the one hand, he was the person who knew us best of all. On the other hand, if he hadn't joined the military, it might have been us who'd walked down that aisle.

"I get it," he says gently. "Relationships aren't easy, and most people can't point to when they shifted off course."

With a sigh, I drag my fingers though my hair. I'm wearing it long these days, and I twirl one strand around my finger idly as I gather my thoughts. "I told you I'd assumed he was having an affair. And maybe he was. But maybe that wasn't it at all, maybe it was because he gotten involved with the wrong people."

"You may have a point. But all that means is that we need to dig into what was going on with him. If it was an affair, whoever he was with might know something. Hell, they might be involved themselves. What made you think that he was cheating? Was there something specific, I mean, that made you think *affair* rather than that he was simply pulling away?" He frowns. "Although I guess there's nothing simple about that."

"There's not," I agree. "But are you telling me

you never saw signs that he was cheating?" It's a question I haven't asked Red before. I'm not sure why not. After all, he's been one of my closest friends for years. And he spent more time with Mel than I did.

So why hadn't I gone to him and asked if he thought my husband was cheating on me? I don't know. Or maybe I do know.

Maybe I didn't care to know the answer.

I realize he hasn't answered, and when I glance over, he's looking right back at me. I swallow, suddenly extremely self-conscious. "Well?" I prod.

"No, I didn't catch any of that kind of vibe. All I knew was that he seemed off, you know?"

"Yeah. I know."

"We need something tangible. We need a place to start looking."

I raise a brow. "Well, we have his phone. Shouldn't we start there?"

He chuckled. "We should, and we will. But it was in their possession, and they had the passcode. So I'm assuming they've already given it a once over."

"You know what they say about assumptions."

He tilts his head in acknowledgement. "True."

"And to be honest, I don't have a better idea. His phone would be my first suggestion. He rarely answered calls if we were together. And if he was on a call when I walked into the room, he'd end it abruptly. Maybe we can look at the numbers he was calling. Or maybe he's got a contact that says Sexy Sidepiece or some such bullshit. After all, he kept his phone locked. Not like I was going to see it, right?"

I realize I've been ranting, my words popping out of my mouth with the force of my anger.

"All good points," he says. "In fact, that may be why they gave me the phone and didn't just send the video."

"Because they think one of us might notice something odd, whereas they might overlook it?"

"It's as good a guess as any."

"So what should we do? Go sit on the sofa and start paging through it?"

"Yes," he says. "But not now. We need to get some sleep. And I want to go to Stark Security in the morning."

"The alarm system," I say. "They shouldn't have been able to disable the safety protocols so easily."

"That, but also the phone."

I shake my head, not understanding.

"If they can do an exact clone of it, you and I can both have a copy to review and compare notes on. And I'll ask them to run all the incoming and outgoing phone numbers through their databases to see if anything pops."

"Got it."

"If nothing else, we should pretty quickly have a sense of whether the phone is a dead end on leads or not. But even if we find something actionable, it's still only one branch of the plan."

I nod, liking the way he's thinking methodically. It makes me feel in my element. After working as a legal assistant at a law firm for the last seven years, I've gained an understanding of how much you can accomplish if you stay focused on your lane.

"So the other branch is the hotel."

He reaches out and taps the end of my nose, something he used to do in college. I pretended like it irritated me, but it never had. What had irritated was that it was his *only* touch. At least until that one night when—

"—the files."

I clear my throat, hoping my cheeks aren't bright red. "Sorry. What?"

"If he really was using a comped room at his friend's hotel, that's someone we should talk to. Can you check the client files and get us a name?"

"I shouldn't—not without clearing it with my boss—but I will."

"Good."

"Right. Okay. I'll go into the office tomorrow. I need to tell them about Mel, anyway."

"And you need to take a week's leave."

I swallow and nod. Under normal circumstances, I'd be surrounded by family and friends for
the next week or so as I planned my husband's
memorial and tried to get myself centered.

As it is, I'm going to spend the time I should be
mourning playing private detective. And to be
honest, I'm okay with that. I'm not someone who
can sit and wallow in grief or pain or loss. I need to
do something.

If I can't bring him back, then maybe I can at
least find answers.

"And then we go to the hotel," I say, continuing
down this path.

"Yes, but we can talk about that tomorrow once
we know we have an address. For all you know, the
guy never actually called for consult, much less
hired the firm."

He has a point. "In that case, what will we do?"

To my surprise, Red laughs. "We worry about
that tomorrow." He stands, holding a hand to help
me up. "We both need rest."

"It's not that late."

"Do you want me to refresh your drink? Might
help you sleep."

I should say no. I've had enough already. But I
can feel the weight of the day in my bones, and I
know how elusive sleep will be. "Yeah," I say. "A
whiskey would be great."

But when he goes to the bar and meets me at my bedroom door with a glass, I can't help but think that it's not liquid comfort I crave, but the warm solace of falling asleep in his arms.

CHAPTER SEVEN

Sure enough, I toss in bed, unable to fall asleep despite the whiskey and the long, hot shower I took before sliding between the sheets. I'd thought a shower and washing my hair would clear my head, but it didn't work. No matter what I try to think about, I can't shake the image of Mel's face being submerged over and over and over in that tub.

I keep my lips pressed tight together to keep my whimpers to myself. Before, I'd been able to skirt this reality, foregoing thinking about what happened to the man I'd once loved enough to marry by burying my thoughts in the details of how to find the killer.

But we're not planning now. We're supposed to be resting. Sleeping. But it's in the dark that demons come. Not the supernatural kind, but the

ones that live in your thoughts and haunt your
dreams.

Stop it. Just stop it!

I roll over, smooshing up my pillow as I try to
get comfortable. Red's not asleep either. Even
though the guest bath separates my bedroom from
his, I can still hear the low rumble of whatever he's
watching on television.

I half-smile, remembering all the late nights in
college. He and Red and I shared an apartment for
sophomore and junior years, then part of our senior
year, too, before Red decided to graduate early and
join the military.

Those days are among my favorites. Study
sessions with popcorn and root beer, then week-
ends with the real thing. We'd watch movies and
hang out or just sit and talk for ages, especially me
and Red. Mel used to fall asleep on the sofa, but
Red and I could analyze a movie to death. For that
matter, we could talk pretty much anything to
death.

Back then I hadn't an inkling that I'd end up
married to Mel. I loved him, of course, but I'd loved
Red, too. They'd been friends since high school in
Texas, and they'd rescued me freshman year when
I was trying to balance on crutches and carry my
books. Even better, they hadn't laughed when I'd
explained how I'd ended up on crutches in the first
place—by ignominiously tumbling off a curb when

I'd seen Bruce Willis walking straight toward me in Santa Monica.

They'd been my friends—nothing more. Especially not Mel. How could I think about him romantically when I'd had a secret crush on Red?

That, of course, was never meant to be.

I toss and turn, trying to get comfortable. Trying to erase the memories and the regrets so that I can finally get some sleep. At some point, I must have dozed off, because when I float up to consciousness again, the television is off and the room is dark and silent.

I roll over and check my phone, expecting it to be almost morning. Instead, it's barely past two. I groan, then lay back again, trying to drift off. But once more, sleep eludes me, my mind too filled with a cacophony of thoughts.

I feel lost. Alone. I'm sad for my husband, and I already miss him terribly. Not in a way that makes me regret asking for the divorce, but because he was a good man who was my friend and now someone has taken him from the world. From me. From everyone who loved him.

I sigh, realizing that in the morning I have to call his parents, and I hate that I can't tell them the truth, because they would undoubtedly want the police involved.

The whole thing is so horrible, and I can't stop thinking about death and darkness. I feel like I'm tumbling into a dark pit full of horrible thoughts and gnashing demons biting at my heels.

I hug myself wishing I was stronger, but I'm not. And I really don't think I can do this alone.

With tears stinging my eyes, I sit up, then slip out of bed and walk the short distance to the guest room. I tap lightly, but when there's no answer I enter anyway. A bit of light seeps in from the crack in the curtains, the illumination coming from the front porch light.

It's not much, but enough that I can see that Red's asleep. I hesitate, knowing I should probably turn around and go back to my room. But that means going back to being alone.

So instead, I move quietly to the bed and slide in beside him. Despite my stealth, I see his body tense the moment I disturb the covers. I'm not surprised. He's always been a light sleeper. On top of that, even though we weren't supposed to know about it, Red once told me and Mel that he'd been part of a Special Forces team. An elite, secret team. And I imagine that living with that kind of danger gives you an even sharper sense of your surroundings.

"It's me," I whisper. "I don't want to be alone. I promise I won't hog the covers."

He rolls over, his eyes on mine, and I'm suddenly aware of how long his lashes are. Not to mention the fact that in turning, the sheet has shifted, settling down around his hips.

My mouth goes dry. I hope—*do I really?*—that he's wearing boxers or something, but maybe I should have considered that before climbing into bed. As it is, his top half is entirely bare, and even in the dim light, I can see the wild and colorful tattoo that dominates his chest.

With effort, I drag my eyes up from it back to his face. "I can stay?"

"Whatever you need, Jo." He reaches out and brushes his thumb lightly over the curve of my cheek. "Anything at all."

I smile and whisper thanks. Then I close my eyes and sleep finally creeps up on me. I start to drift away, and as I do, my mind returns to the single kiss that we shared after he came back from that horrible mission that he refused to talk about. The last mission before he left the service. And though I don't know for sure, I assume that's the reason he left.

It was still months before Mel and I got romantically involved, and the three of us had been laughing and watching a stupid movie. I don't even remember what. Mel left to go pick up more beer, and the vibe shifted to something edgier. Needier. I hadn't expected it at all, but when it did, I knew that it was what I'd wanted. I don't think he'd planned it either, but when I leaned toward him to reach the remote, he cupped my chin and turned my face toward him.

I'd been breathless almost to the point of begging. An eternity seemed to hang between us, our eyes locked on each other. Then he pulled me to him and kissed me like I'd never been kissed before. Or, honestly, like I've never been kissed since.

A long kiss, so deep and sweet and passionate that it seemed to steal my senses. I was floating in space, and I never wanted it to end.

Who am I kidding? *Not end?* Hell, I wanted *more.*

But all too soon he pushed me away, breathing hard. "I'm sorry," he said. "That was a mistake."

"No," I said. "I don't think it was. I think it was incredible."

I smiled, but his expression didn't change, and I felt the tension grow in my chest.

"It won't happen again." He stood up, then walked to the door. He paused there, and all he said was, "Jo, I'm sorry. I don't think I'll ever be able to tell you how sorry I am."

And then he left, leaving me on the couch, my lips still tingling, and my mind spinning with confusion.

We never spoke of it again and I wasn't sure if I was hurt or angry or just confused. I ended up deciding on the latter, because I didn't have any other choice. He was my best friend. He'd just gotten back from an assignment that I knew nothing about other than that it had been like going through hell.

I had no idea what was going on with him emotionally. And I knew that, more than anything else, he deserved the benefit of the doubt. I could let it go, even if, in my deepest most secret places, I held it close every night for the rest of my life.

Over the next months, the topic turned to the dream of starting a distillery, and we three were together almost constantly as those plans evolved. Every day, I hoped something else would spark between Red and me, and every night I was disappointed.

I'd sit a little too close, then accidentally brush his hand. I knew I shouldn't, but I couldn't help it. If he noticed, he never commented. And he never kissed me again.

Soon enough, I let it drop, though I still kept the memory in my heart. Not long after that, Mel started to see me as more than a friend, and I leaned into that. I even went so far as to ask Red if he minded that Mel and I might start dating.

I told myself that I wasn't asking because of the kiss. On the contrary, it was because we'd been a trifecta of friends, and if Mel and I hooked up, it might make it strange.

Except of course it was about the kiss. It was always about that kiss.

But all Red said was that we'd make a great couple and he wished us well.

That was the day my fantasy of having Red in my arms finally died.

Now, as I drift off to sleep, I can't help but wonder what would have happened if, on that day long ago, instead of wishing us well, Red had pulled me close and kissed me.

CHAPTER EIGHT

R ed bolted awake with a startled yowl, his heart thudding painfully in his chest as he leapt out of bed, desperate to escape the hell he'd awakened to: an erection, a woman in his bed, and the earthy smell of juniper and eucalyptus filling his senses.

No, no, goddammit, no!

"Red? Red, Christ, are you okay?"

The dark fog around him faded to reveal the reality that the woman in his bed wasn't *her*. It was Jo, looking both concerned and terrified.

His cock tightened, and he was breathing hard, trying to rein it in. It would be so easy. Push her back against the mattress. Hold her wrists above her head with one hand as he fucked her hard, his other hand over her mouth to stifle her moans until he let her cry out.

He wanted that, damn him. Wanted to over-power. To take.

To take back.

He wanted to hear her call his name, to beg for more, to have her completely at his mercy.

He wanted it, dammit.

And there was no way in hell he was going down that rabbit hole with Jo.

"*Red.*"

A sharp swath of anger—at himself, at his demons—cut through him, and he bent over, his palms to his knees as he tried to breathe. To center himself. *He was home. He'd escaped. The bitch was dead. A painful memory, but still just a memory.*

"Red? You're scaring me."

"Just give me a damn second, okay?" He shouldn't snap, especially not at Jo. It wasn't her fault he was fucked up. Broken. A victim to his goddamn past.

He looked up to tell her as much, feeling like an ass when he saw the concern reflected in her eyes.

She was propped up on one arm, but now she sat upright, the sheet falling away as she did to reveal pert nipples under the thin tank top she wore. His cock grew harder, his vision swimming with violent need. *She didn't have a clue. Not a goddamn clue.*

It would be so easy to take her. To *use* her. To push past this moment so he could center himself.

He took a step forward, then stopped cold, sickened by his own base needs.

"I'm sorry. Fuck it, I'm sorry." The words came out as a growl, and he turned, barely registering Jo's worried and confused expression as he stalked out of the room and into the guest bath.

He turned on the shower, then sat on the edge of the tub, stupidly wishing that things were different. That *he* was different.

He remembered that first day he'd met her when she'd tumbled off a curb, unstable on her crutches. He'd leapt to her rescue, then held her close as she regained her balance. Her hair had smelled of strawberries, and that combined with the sensation of her body pressed against him had made him giddy.

He'd wanted her that day.

Hell, he'd wanted her every day after, too. But he never made a move. How could he when he and Mel and Jo had so quickly bonded, their friendship the kind that he'd known even then would last for years? Something rock solid that he could count on.

No way would he risk screwing that up.

Then he'd graduated early to join the military and had been immediately recruited by the SOC. His perspective had shifted in those early days in the service, forging in him a deep need for stability and love, home and hearth.

He'd tried not to think of Jo in those days—by

then she was firmly in the friend slot. But he'd
gotten serious with a few women he'd met either on
missions or in those months when he was off-duty,
recharging for the next deployment. And somehow,
in the back of his mind, he always compared them
to Jo. Made sense, after all. Sex wasn't everything;
if he was going to sleep with a woman, he'd wanted
her to be a friend, too.

Lisa had been both. Lover, friend. A kind
woman with a sharp mind, a brutal uppercut, and
deadly accuracy with a firearm. They'd worked two
missions together before she'd gone undercover as a
flight attendant.

Before everything had changed.

Before *he'd* changed.

Now Lisa was dead and Red wasn't the man he
used to be, not by a long shot.

More than that, he knew he never would be.
He'd tried to find himself after Romania. Tried to
slide back into this life and normalcy. Hell, he'd
even turned to Jo, certain that if anyone could bring
him fully back to himself, it was her.

God, how he'd wanted her.

He'd held back at first, hesitant to poison their
friendship. But there was no denying that the
passion he'd always felt for her hadn't dimmed.
He'd taken a risk that night by kissing her, and his
heart had leapt when she'd responded with such

passion, almost with desperation. As if she'd been waiting years for his touch.

Hell, maybe she had been. Hadn't he? Even though he'd forced himself to do nothing, hadn't he always wanted her?

God yes, and for a few blissful moments, he'd lost himself in the sweetness of her lips and the strawberry scent of her hair.

It didn't last, though. He should have known better. The ghosts. The panic. The weight on his lungs and heart so heavy he couldn't breathe.

He'd broken away, feeling like an ass but knowing it didn't matter. He had to get some distance between them. Had to make her understand that nothing could ever happen.

She deserved better than a man like him, broken now in so many ways. And there was no way in hell he would bring her down to that level.

But oh how he wanted to.

To claim her. Make her his. Feel her alive and wild and vibrant beneath him, begging him. Needing him.

He wanted that release. Craved that sensation of being alive.

And what in his life had ever made him feel more alive than simply being in Jo's presence? No one, not even Lisa.

But he couldn't have her, and he damn well knew it, so why the hell was he torturing himself?

And what the fuck was he doing even thinking like that less than a day after his best friend's murder?

It didn't matter. His mind had no conscience, and in his thoughts his mouth was on her tight nipple, his fingers sliding between her legs. And his cock—

"Red?" Her voice and a tentative knock, and he shot guiltily to his feet, only then realizing how steamy the bathroom had become. "Are you okay?"

He almost laughed. Did it seem like he was okay? But he said nothing. She tried two more times, then gave up. He closed his eyes and counted to ten, hating himself for craving her like that. For having the images in his head even now. Her naked body beneath him, open to him. His to use like a shield against the demons that haunted him.

They'd made him a damn monster.

With a sigh of self-loathing, he stripped, then stepped into the shower. He tilted his head back, wishing the water could wash away the pain and the past. It couldn't, though. Romania had scarred him. Hell, it had destroyed him. Lisa and his team and those other two innocent women had died. He'd lived. But to this day, he wondered if they hadn't gotten the better deal.

He stayed under the spray until the water turned cold, then felt like an ass about that, too. Jo probably wanted to shower as well.

When he couldn't justify staying in the bathroom any longer, he wrapped one of the huge towels around his hips and left the bathroom for the guest room, hoping to hell Jo wasn't in there.

She wasn't, and he breathed a sigh of relief, then smiled when he saw the folded clothes on the bed. He'd been an absolute prick, but she'd still thought to bring him fresh clothes.

He put them on—jeans and a Swift Red tee— then told himself he couldn't avoid seeing her and pulled open the door. She looked up when he entered the living area, and he was relieved to see she'd put on a robe. She stood in the connecting kitchen, staring at the coffeemaker as if that would make it brew faster.

She looked up at him, and though she smiled in greeting, he thought he saw trepidation in her eyes. As if she was afraid he'd go postal on her again.

"I thought Mel's clothes might fit you. Figured you'd want something clean."

"Thanks." He shoved his hands in his pockets. "Sorry."

"It's fine."

It wasn't fine, not by a long shot. But he didn't argue.

She poured a cup of coffee and passed it to him. "Do you want to talk about it?"

"No."

Her lips twitched. "Color me not surprised." She crossed the small area back to the coffee maker.

"Bottom line, I'm not used to waking up to a woman in my bed." That was true, but it damn sure wasn't all of it, and he was certain Jo would realize that as well.

She poured her own coffee with her back to him, then turned to face him. "Are you telling me you're celibate? Or you just haven't been dating for a while?"

He almost told her it didn't matter. He'd apologized; end of story. But dammit, she deserved more. This was Jo, after all, and even if he couldn't have her, that didn't alter the reality that he'd loved her for years. As a friend and, yes, as so much more.

He took a sip of coffee. "I don't date. And I'm not celibate."

Her head tilted as she took that in, and he wondered if she understood. He *had* dated when they were in school, and it was only his fear of screwing up their friendship that had kept Jo out of that circle. But since he'd returned? There was only a certain type of woman he was willing to let see the kind of man he was now.

"Call girls? Jesus, Red, why? You're an incredible man. I can think of a half dozen women who'd be thrilled to go out with you."

"I sincerely doubt that."

"What are you—"

"We're dropping it, okay?" He'd already skirted

too close to the line. He had no intention of ever telling her what happened, and if they kept this conversation up, he'd have to either lie or hurt her feelings to shut it down. "You're my closest friend in the world, Jo, but that doesn't mean I owe you an explanation."

She pressed her lips together, and he felt like an ass.

"No," she said after a long pause. "Of course it doesn't. I'm sorry about pushing. And about coming to bed. I should have stayed in my room, not expected you to babysit me."

She was right; he should never have let her share his bed. That had opened the door, and now his secrets were trying to escape. But how could he have refused her?

"Last night wasn't about my issues," he said. "It was about you and Mel and loss, and there was no way in hell I was going to push you away. I will always be there for you, Jo. Especially right now. Please tell me you know that? That even though I lost my shit, you still believe it."

She looked down at her coffee as she said, "Of course I do. It's all really stressful now. We should cut ourselves some slack."

Everything she said made sense, but there was too clean an edge to her voice, as if they were strangers finding their way.

She took one last sip of her coffee, then put her

mug in the sink. "I'm going to go get dressed. Then we can head out."

"Sounds good."

She brushed past him as she left, his body shifting into fight-or-flight mode as she did, a visceral response to that wretched shampoo scent.

He watched her leave, wishing things were different. Wishing *he* was different. But they weren't, and when she reached her bedroom door, he called out for her to stop.

She paused, looking at him over her shoulder.

"Do me a favor and take a shower, would you?"

Her brows rose. "Excuse me?"

"The shampoo, Jo. Just do me this one fucking favor and use a different shampoo."

Her eyes flickered with a thousand questions, but she didn't voice them, and for that he was grateful. Instead, all she said was, "Sure."

Then she disappeared into the room, and he dropped his head to his hands, grateful for that one, small, stupid victory.

Damien wasn't at Stark Security when they arrived, a fact that surprised Red. His brother had told him that after Damien had played the bad ass action hero role in New York, he'd decided to take a more active role in Stark Security. After all, it was a

venture that he felt strongly about, having founded
the organization in the wake of his daughter's
kidnapping.

"He's here pretty often these days," the
agency's chief, Ryan Hunter, told Red when he
said as much. "But he still has a universe to run. I
think he's in Boston for the day. Possibly Amster-
dam." He shrugged. "He's a hard man to keep up
with. Come on, let's get settled in one of the conference rooms. It's good to see you both again," he
added, nodding to Jo, "but I'm terribly sorry about
the circumstances."

A tall, lean man with chestnut hair and vivid
blue eyes, Ryan crossed the room with long,
purposeful strides, barely even pausing as he
answered questions tossed at him from various
agents and support personnel at the stations that
dotted the room.

Their destination was a large, glass-enclosed
conference room on the west side of the building.
One side opened out over the agency's interior, the
other over the courtyard of The Domino, a rela-
tively new business park in Santa Monica that had
been completed as a co-venture between Damien
and his brother Jackson Steele.

Red walked to the far wall, looking out over the
people gathered at the coffee cart, sitting on
benches, enjoying a bit of the morning outdoors as
they took a break from their work. He envied them,

but he pushed the emotion aside. For all he knew, each and every one of them was broken, their scars as deeply hidden as his.

"Can they see in?" Jo asked. "I mean, don't you guys do all sorts of secret stuff in here?"

"We do, though I don't imagine anyone would find a meeting around a conference table to be that revealing."

"Lip reading," Red said. "You should have me or Renly give it a test run sometime. I bet we'd leave that courtyard with dozens of your secrets."

"A good point," Ryan said, knowing full well that both Red and Renly were proficient at lip-reading and ASL, having learned when their mother lost her hearing. "But the truth is that the glass is one-way only. And when we do have sensitive meetings in here, we black it out entirely to be absolutely certain. Not to mention that the view can be distracting."

As if in demonstration, he pushed a button on a control panel located at the head of the huge table. Immediately, the glass shifted from clear to opaque.

"Neat trick," Jo said.

"We aim to please." Ryan gestured. "Go ahead and grab a seat. Renly and the others will join us in a moment."

As if on cue, the door opened and Renly entered with Mario, who Red remembered as the agency's resident tech genius right behind him.

"Did you and Damien fill everyone in?" Red asked his brother.

"Yup," Renly said.

"We took a quick look last night," Mario said. "You were right to be wary of multiple surveillance devices. So now we're setting up to do a more thorough sweep for any audio or visual bugs or hacks, so we can log and map them all, hopefully do a backtrace. Plus we'll install a full upgrade on your system. As for the bugs, for now, we'd like to keep anything we find in place, with the exception of the camera in the fermentation room."

"Why take that one?" Jo asked.

"Because Red knows it's there," Renly said. "We take that because you're smart and figured it out. But we leave the others so our bad guys think they're clever."

"I can live with that," Red said.

"How do you want us to handle it if we find surveillance in your homes?"

Beside him, Jo leaned forward. "Do you really think that will happen?"

"Won't know until we know," Mario said.

She leaned back, biting her lower lip. Red reached over and took her hand. Their eyes met— just one quick glance—but the awkwardness was gone, thank God, and they seemed to be back where they should be.

"So you just need us for surveillance and security?" Ryan asked.

"For now," Red confirmed. He glanced at Jo. "Right now, we only have one lead as to who might have done this. We're going to follow it up today."

"Happy to go with you, bro," Renly said, but Red shook his head.

"The hell you will. I don't even know why you're here. I thought you and Abby were taking the week off to get her moved into your place and clear your plates before the wedding."

"That's still on the agenda, but if you expect me—"

"I do expect it," Red said. "Don't get me wrong. I appreciate any help you want to offer. But this is your time, man. Enjoy it. And I'll see you for drinks on Thursday. Open bar at Swift Red in lieu of a strip club for your bachelor party. Very untraditional of you, bro."

"Abby's all I want an eyeful of," Renly said. "And I can still marry my girl and help you out."

"No way," Jo said. "Red's right. We've got this. And if we need help, Ryan will put someone on it, right?" She glanced toward Ryan, who nodded.

Renly shook his head. "I hate the thought of—"

"I have six minutes on you, bro," Red said. "So shut the hell up and do what your older brother says."

"Ass," Renly replied, but Red knew that was the end of it.

"Thank you all so much," Jo said, writing down the code for the keypad lock at her house and sliding it to Mario.

"Like I need a code to get in. Oh, sorry," he added, probably seeing the look of shock on Jo's face. "Fact of life, though, right? But I'll upgrade the keypad while I'm there, too. And you double-lock with a deadbolt, right?"

She nodded.

"If I can get it open in under twenty seconds, I'll replace that, too. I've got a model in the supply room I'll take with us," he added, as if he was certain the existing lock would fail. From what little Red had heard about the tech geek's skills, Red was certain Jo would have a new set of locks by the time they returned to her place.

"Yours too," Mario said, looking at Red. "Wanna give me your key or code?"

Red half-grinned. "Hell no. If you need that to get in, you're not anywhere near qualified to be on this project."

They all laughed, and it felt good, the last of the tension that had been clinging to him finally fading away.

"You're sure there's nothing else we can help you with now?" Ryan asked as he pushed back from the table and stood.

"Actually, I forgot one thing." He pulled out Mel's phone and put it on the table. "We need this cloned and analyzed."

Mario reached for it. "You got the code, or do I need to hack it?"

"Got it," Red said, then recited it from memory.

"Two clones? That way we've got one for each of you and we'll keep the original here. If we're looking for oddities to try to figure out what Mel got himself into, Jo's gonna be the best bet, but this way, we'll all have eyes on."

"Perfect," Red said.

"We're on it," Ryan said. "Anything else?"

"I think that's it for now," Jo said. "But with any luck, we'll have a few more leads by this evening that we'll will need help with."

"Call me tonight," Renly said, and Red promised to do just that.

Then, knowing that at the very least, the distillery and their homes would be secure, Red put a hand to Jo's back and steered her toward the door.

Time to go play detective.

CHAPTER NINE

"You remember how to get to the firm?" I ask, once we're away from The Domino.

"Straight up Santa Monica toward the towers, but you'll have to remind me of the turn."

"Sure." I pick at non-existent lint on the knee of my favorite jeans, hating how stilted and awkward we sound, and not really sure how that happened. We'd both been quiet on the ride to Stark Security, but inside the office, things felt back to normal. Or, at least, what passes for normal at the moment.

Now, though, it seems like I've lost him again, and I want to understand why.

I hesitate, then tell myself to go for it. The worst that happens is that he shuts me out, and he's going to do that anyway. "So, um," I begin. "What's the deal with my shampoo?"

He doesn't answer immediately, but I see his

hands tighten on the steering wheel, his knuckles going white.

"Never mind," I say. "It's no big deal. I only wondered why—"

"Bad memories," he says, taking his eyes off the road just long enough to glance at me. "And we're going to leave it at that."

"Sure. No problem."

We drive in silence some more, slightly less awkward this time, and I almost smile when we stop at a red light and he asks me, "So why'd you stop using the strawberry stuff anyway?"

"I didn't. Well, yeah, I did, but only yesterday. Crazy timing, huh?"

"And the why?"

I have no idea why this fascinates him so much, but maybe he's just making conversation to get past the awkwardness, too, and if that's the case, I'm all in. "A friend is a rep for an organic beauty supply company. She gave me a sample."

"Hmm. Well, don't use it. Go back to the strawberries."

"I will." What I really want to say is that he needs to open up, if not to me, then to somebody. I mean, when a shampoo triggers that kind of a response, there's some serious shit going on.

I don't tell him any of that, though. Instead, I say, "You can talk to me, you know."

He doesn't look my direction, but he does say, "Yeah. I know."

I wait for him to elaborate, and that doesn't happen either. I consider pushing, but that won't end well. So instead, I sit back in my seat, resigned to driving in silence.

"Why did you marry Mel?"

The question comes completely out of the blue, and my instinctive response rests right there on the tip of my tongue. Practical words about friendship and love and building a life.

Instead, I hear myself saying, "I didn't want to be alone."

He glances sideways at me. "Your mom."

It's a statement, not a question, because of course Red knows me well. I shrug. "Probably."

"You're not alone, Jo. You never have been."

He may be right about that, but that's because I've worked so damn hard after those early years. I'd been seven when my father walked away, and I haven't heard or seen from him since. I barely remember him, and I assume he's dead. At the very least, he's dead to me.

From that day, it was just my mom and me struggling to get by. Her a single mom with no family, me a little kid terrified that she was going to leave one day, too.

And then, of course, she did.

I know it wasn't her fault. It's not like she asked for leukemia. But she's gone all the same, and at twelve I really didn't understand that. Intellectually, sure. I was a bright enough kid. But emotionally? I was a wreck, and I blamed her for leaving. For the fact that I ended up in foster care. Some families were okay, and a couple were terrible. But I never felt like I belonged. I was the outsider. The one who had to be taken care of.

Which was why I graduated early and started college. I'd thrown my pain and my grief into my grades, as if getting straight-As would somehow make me worthy. Could help me find a real family.

In a way, I guess it did. I found Mel and Red, after all.

The truth is, if Red had stayed in town, I might not have married Mel. I loved him—I did. In the same way I loved Red. They were my best friends, my closest confidants. And when it was the three of us, I felt like I *did* have a family.

But then things started to shift. My attraction to Red that I'd always managed to shove to the background kept teasing me. And then that night when we kissed—well, it mattered to me.

So much that when he pushed me away, I felt more alone than ever. And Mel, bless him, was always so sweet to me. Our friendship had always been intense, and when he confessed that he wanted to shift what we had toward something romantic, it made sense to me. I already loved him, after all.

It had been a mistake, of course. We were meant to be friends, he and I, and although I almost believed our lie, over time, the illusion shattered. I craved what we used to have, and I think Mel did too.

But more than that, I craved Red, too. And not just in a friendly way.

Honestly, is it any wonder Mel had an affair?

A flicker of anger teases my senses, because the truth is, I *didn't* have an affair. More, I tried to talk to him about it. Hell, I *did* talk to him about it, and he even agreed that something had changed after we married. We'd lost that friends-connection we'd had, and there'd been nothing deeper to take its place.

I suggested counseling. I suggested talking.

In the end, I suggested a divorce.

He wasn't having any of it. That's when I saw an attorney. And by that time, I was certain something was up. An affair, I assumed. And that only pissed me off more.

Now, it breaks my heart that those years poisoned our friendship. And that I was so terribly complicit. If only I'd said no when he put marriage on the table. If only I hadn't been so desperate to not be alone.

I married Mel to save myself from that fate. But in the end, I was more alone than ever.

"Hey," Red says, pulling my attention back from my misery. "I lose you?"

I shake my head. "Just thinking about being alone. Somehow it always comes around again."

He takes my hand, then squeezes. "Bullshit. You've got me, right? And we're going to find out who killed your husband."

"*Our* friend," I stress. Because to me, those were the best years, and the ones I want to keep close in my memories.

"Hell, yes," Red says, then pulls his hand away, returning it to the steering wheel. I mourn the loss, but it's probably for the best. With Red, my thoughts seem to have a mind of their own, and it's a pretty naughty mind.

I shift sideways so that I can see him better. We used to talk about everything. Now I'm holding back about my rocky marriage and my lust for him, and he's holding back about what happened overseas.

I know things have changed, and we're not college friends whose biggest problem is getting notes for all the lectures we skipped. But I still miss that intimacy. Those long nights where the three of us drank and talked and shared our dreams and our secrets. And, yes, our fears.

"Will you ever tell me what happened?" I ask,

the question out before I have sense enough to call it back.

"Happened?"

I scoff. "I'm not an idiot, Charlie Cooper. You came back with a shit ton of baggage. It weighs you down. I can see it. Hell, even before this morning, I could see it."

"Christ, Jo, do we—"

I hold up a hand, cutting off his sharp words. "It's me, Red. Remember me? We used to be able to talk about anything."

"And then you married Mel."

"I—" I go silent. I have no idea what that has to do with anything. "In case you missed the memo, you son-of-a-bitch, I'm not married now. And what the hell does that have to do with anything anyway?"

We're at a light, and he turns to look at me. His expression is unreadable. But his eyes—oh, God, I know the nature of that heat in his eyes. I'd seen it before on that night we shared a kiss. The night when he pushed me away.

I swallow a gasp, suddenly unsure of everything. "We need to talk."

"No," he says. "We really don't."

I don't argue. What would be the point? Instead, we drive in silence, heading to Century City and the law offices of Kline and Rosenfeld, until I point out where to turn, then guide him into the parking structure. I pass him my access card, and we find an empty space after going in circles for about ten minutes. Only the lawyers have assigned parking. Legal assistants and other support staff get to battle it out among the other tenants and guests.

On the whole though, I like working here. The building is nice and the people are demanding only when the work requires it. Nobody's an ass just to be one, and considering what some of my friends at other firms put up with, I consider that a major plus.

Not only that, but it's walking distance to the mall, which means decent food and shopping during my lunch hour.

We take the elevator to twenty-eight, but before I can step toward the firm's double doors, Red takes my elbow and tugs me back.

"I'm sorry," he says.

I hadn't realized how tense I was until I hear those words. I exhale, then give him a hug. "I'm sorry, too."

"Are we good?" he asks as I pull away.

"Absolutely." I can't guarantee I won't press him again later, but for right now my heart is full again, knowing that my best friend is beside me.

We cross the small alcove, and Red holds the glass doors, etched with the firm name, open for me.

Immediately, our receptionist, Roxie, stands. She comes out from behind her desk, then pulls me into a hug. Well-past retirement age, Roxie has been with the firm longer than anyone, including the partners, as neither the original Kline or Rosenfeld are still alive. It's like being hugged by a loving grandmother, and it's everything I can do not to burst into tears.

"We didn't expect to see you this week."

"I know." I'd called this morning to tell the attorney I'm assigned to about Mel's death. "But I can't just sit at home. Red's taking me to deal with probate stuff," I lie, "so I thought I could pick up some files and do a little work at home."

"Oh, sugar—"

"I need to do something."

She gives me another quick hug, then nods. "Do you want me to tell the partners you're here?"

I shake my head. "They'll be in a staff meeting now. I'll just grab a few things and go."

"Well, okay, but you let us know if you need anything. And you take care of her, Charlie."

"I will, ma'am."

Roxie is the only person I know who regularly calls Red by his legal name. They met when Red came in to sign the corporate documents for Swift Red that my boss had put together.

I lead Red back to my office, accepting condolences along the way. I share the space with two other legal assistants, neither of whom are here. "Probably in the meeting," I say, nodding for Red to close the door.

The first order of business is to see if we ever took on Mel's hotel friend as a client, and once I'm logged in, I navigate to the admin section and pull up the client list.

"Are you authorized to be in those files?" Red asks, though since I'm already in, the question is somewhat moot.

"Technically, no. But I'm not logged in as me."

"Jo..."

I look up at him. "I did some work with Marissa a few months ago," I say, referring to the office manager. "I saw her type in her password." I have a knack for remembering certain things. Not a photographic memory per se, but names and numbers have a habit of sticking with me.

"So it will look like she was in the files."

"Assuming anyone even notices. It's hardly top-secret stuff."

"But if they do, won't they notice it's from your computer?"

I shake my head. "Not unless they dig deep. And seriously, aren't you overthinking this? We're not doing a secret mission trying to get enemy intel. This is just your run of the mill law firm, and all we're looking for is a name."

"Fair enough. Too many years running black ops. But hurry, okay?"

"That's the plan."

As he leans over me, his nose near my ear, I try to focus on my search. But his proximity is distracting. As is the certainty that he can smell my strawberry shampoo. I still don't understand why changing back was important to him, but considering his mood this morning, I decide not to explore the topic.

Besides, I've just gotten a hit. "There, see?" I point to the screen where Mel's name is prominent. "He's referred five clients over the last three years. I know Jack and Remy," I add. "We met them after college when you were overseas. Looks like they're currently inactive, which makes sense. Both have moved to the East coast."

"Donna Clark is a frequent customer at the distillery," Red tells me. "A party planner."

I swivel around to look at him, my eyes narrowing. "Were they affectionate?"

He frowns. "Unless she's the coolest female on the planet, she didn't have a thing going on with Mel. And as far as I know, she's happily married." He sighs. "Then again, I assumed you and Mel were, too."

I look away, shrugging uncomfortably. "Yeah, well. Nobody ever really knows anybody, do they?"

"No," he says. "They don't."

I tilt my head up to look at him. "Most people tell me I'm a horrible pessimist when I say that."

"I'm not most people."

For a moment, it feels as if the air has been sucked from my lungs. Then I'm forced to draw a breath, and the moment evaporates, leaving me to wonder if it had been there at all.

"Here are the last two. Patrick Kline and Martin Corveau. Either ring a bell?"

He shakes his head.

"Then we go further." I click on Patrick first, only to discover that he's deceased. "That leaves Martin. Cross your fingers." I hit the button to open up his information, then hear Red whisper, "Bingo."

He's right. From what little I can see on the intake file, Corveau made a significant amount of money investing in a tech startup, then used it to buy a hotel about nine months ago.

"The Hollywood Terrace," Red reads. "He would have gotten a good deal."

"You know it?"

"Not directly. There were some stories in the news. Stark Security was involved, actually, though that part wasn't public. Apparently some bigwig bought it, fixed it up, then used it for high-end prostitution. And worse. He lost it, it sat empty, and then it was bought up recently."

"By our Mr. Corveau. Concidence, or do you

think he's dirty? And if so, how? What are we even dealing with?"

"I haven't got a clue." He tapped the screen. "Until now. What do you say I buy you a drink at one of old Hollywood's poshest hotels?"

CHAPTER TEN

"This is seriously impressive," Jo said as they stepped inside the Art Deco lobby of the historic Hollywood Terrace Hotel. "The former owner really held wild sex parties here?"

Red shrugged. "So Ryan tells me. Apparently Quincy met Eliza at one. Or, rather, they met again." He'd met Quince, the former MI6 agent through Renly, as he'd met several of the Stark Security operatives. But keeping track of their various adventures was a job in and of itself.

He took a step forward, only to realize that he'd lost Jo. He turned back, amused by the perplexed expression on her face.

"What?"

"Granted I only met them that one time when they came with Renly for drinks at Swift Red, and they looked head-over-heels in love. But are you telling me they actually met at a sex party?"

He had to laugh, and almost considered leading her on, weaving a steamy and decadent story before giving in and telling her the truth. It was something he might have done in college. Now, though, with his desire for her so close to the surface, he wasn't about to open that door.

"They were both undercover," he explained.

She snickered. "Oh, I bet they were."

With a laugh of his own, he took her arm. "Come on, let's go see if we can track down Martin Corveau."

They crossed the elegant lobby to the gilt registration desk, then asked to speak to a manager. The woman who came over wore a 1940s-inspired suit, and smiled at them with professional politeness. "Welcome to The Terrace. How may I help you?"

"We'd like to speak to the owner," Jo said. "Martin Corveau. Is he on property?"

"Oh, I see. If there's a problem, I'm sure I can assist you."

"No problem at all. I'm from Kline and Rosenfeld. We were doing an audit of our records and realized that there were a few minor corporate papers that needed updating. As I was going to be in the area anyway, I thought I would come by and save him the trouble."

Red tried not to wince. That wasn't part of the

plan they'd discussed during the drive, and if Corveau called the firm to check, they were sunk. Still, if it worked, it would certainly be the most expeditious way to approach the man, especially if he was dirty and paranoid of strangers.

"I see. One moment." She stepped sideways to a computer hidden behind the reception desk. Red could hear her typing, her professional smile never wavering.

She must have been texting Corveau, because a moment later, she returned with a genuine smile. "If you would like to take a seat in the lobby, Mr. Corveau will be right down."

"Thanks," Jo said, but when she turned away from the desk, her expression shifted from professional to deer-in-the-headlights.

He bit back a grin, took her arm, and led her to a plush settee in the open area.

"I took a risk," she said.

"And it paid off," he said mildly. "Don't do it again."

She winced. "I know. Sorry. I thought of it as we were walking in. I mean, it's the most solid connection, and the safest. If I introduced myself as Mel's wife—well, what if he's the one who sent the thugs to attack me?"

"I agree one-hundred percent." He paused. "Just don't do it again."

"I know. Sorry." She reached over and took his

hand, then squeezed. "We're a team, right?"

For a moment—just one, brief, horrible moment —he wanted to stand up, leave that place, and get as far away from the distillery, Mel's death, and this woman as possible. He did *not* do teams. Not anymore. But damned if she wasn't right. They'd become one so seamlessly he hadn't even noticed. And though that terrified him, he knew it was true. More, there was no way he was walking away now. Not with Jo still in danger.

"Red?"

"Yes," he said quickly. "Yes, of course, we're a team."

"No, I mean you're hurting me."

He realized with a start that he'd tightened his grip on her hand. "Sorry," he said, releasing her.

"You okay?"

There was an edge to her voice, concern mixed with wariness, and he was certain that she was thinking of the way he'd lost his shit that morning. "Fine. Just distracted."

"Well, don't be. I need you on your A-game."

"You're right," he said. "And I am. I won't let you down."

"*We* won't let Mel down," she corrected. "And we won't get killed in the process. Deal?"

He couldn't help but grin. "Deal."

Across the lobby, a tall, thin man in a silver-gray suit exited the elevator, then glanced toward the reception area. The clerk who'd helped them nodded in their direction, and the man, presumably Corveau, strode to them, his expression curious, but not wary. Perhaps he wasn't involved. Or, perhaps, he was very good at hiding his true emotions.

"I'm Martin Corveau," he said as he took the seat opposite them. "I understand you're from Kline and Rosenfeld? Is there a problem? Ms. Painter mentioned something about documents."

"Mr. Corveau, I'm Jo Swift, and I'm a legal assistant at the firm. This is my friend, Charlie Cooper."

"You can call me Red."

Corveau's brow furrowed. "Red Cooper. You're Mel's partner. And you're his wife."

"Yes, sir."

"I see." He leaned back in the chair, then leaned forward again. "No, I'm sorry, I don't see at all."

Jo glanced toward Red, and when he nodded, she drew a breath, then began, launching into the approach they'd previously agreed to take with the man. "I'm very sorry to tell you that my husband is dead. He—well, the truth is he committed suicide yesterday. We're trying to figure out why."

"I'm so sorry to hear that. But I don't under-stand why you're here. You think I might know something?"

Red had been watching the man's face,

searching for any sign of nerves or obfuscation. He
saw nothing.

"The distillery has been doing well," Red said.
"But at the same time, Mel was trying to expand.
We know he'd been negotiating a supply contract
with your hotel, and since he spent so much time in
discussions with you, we thought he might have
said something that can help us understand."

Even before he finished speaking, Red knew
that something was off. The man's brow was
furrowed, and he was slowly shaking his head.
Now, he said, "I'm sorry. I enjoyed Mel's company,
but I didn't know him that well. He approached me
once about a supply contract, I told him I wasn't
interested, and that was that."

Red glanced at Jo, who leaned forward. "You
only saw him the one time? But he introduced you
to the firm."

"Oh, I saw him quite often. He and I met
through a local business-owners' association, and he
often came here at lunch or in the evening for a
drink."

Red's frown deepened. Mel had told Jo they'd
met at a gym. "So you were never in negotiations?"

"Not at all."

"Was there someone else he might have been
negotiating with?" Jo asked.

"I handle those details myself. I'm not Conrad
Hilton. This is the only hotel I own, and I bought it

because I have a love of historic buildings and this one was horribly mistreated by its previous owner. It's my home as well. I keep the penthouse suite, though I travel quite a bit."

"So you'd chat with him if he was here for a drink?" Jo asked.

"Certainly. In passing at least. As I said, we were friendly acquaintances."

"Did he say anything that might give us a clue as to the reason for his death?"

The man slowly shook his head. "I can't think of anything."

"Was he," Jo began, then cleared her throat before starting over. "Could he have been having an affair?"

"Mrs. Swift," Corveau said in a solemn voice, "I wouldn't know. And even if I did, I would hesitate to sully the memory or the reputation of a friend."

"Okay. Thanks," Jo whispered, and Red couldn't tell if she believed him or not.

To him, it sounded like one of the more elusive answers he'd ever heard, and he followed up with a question of his own. "Do you know if Mel held business meetings in the restaurant or bar?"

"Yes, I'm certain of it. I'd see him sometimes and drop by the table to say hello."

"Did he ever introduce you? I'm talking to all of our current business contacts, but if he was negotiating with potential future suppliers, they may not be on my radar."

"I'm afraid not. Or, at least, not that I remember. Honestly, I didn't chat with him here that often. I assumed he'd prefer to be left alone to do his work."

"There was a woman he told me he was negotiating with," Jo adds. "He mentioned liking her enough to possibly invite her over for dinner. Did you happen to notice him with any women at these meetings?"

"One or two. There was a woman I saw him with at least twice, but I don't know her name. She had dark hair that she wore in a twist. I only remember because it reminded me of my wife's style." He shifted to the edge of the seat. "Again, I'm sorry for your loss, and for not being more help. But please feel free to reach out again if you need anything."

"Of course," Red said. "Thank you so much for your time." He waited until Corveau had walked away, then turned to Jo with a smile. "Well, that was productive. We have our first lead. Potentially, anyway."

She made a whooshing motion over her head.

"Security footage. If we can identify the woman, we might be able to identify her."

Jo nodded slowly. "Because if she was his

mistress, she may know something. Something he never told me."

"It's possible," Red said. "It's also possible that whoever killed Mel knows about her. She might even have the package, or they might believe she does. Which means she may be in as much danger as we are."

"Oh, hell." Jo's curse was soft, and she whacked the heel of her hand against her forehead. "I'm such a bitch. I was thinking only that she was screwing my husband—the husband I'd already asked to divorce me for more reasons than a possible affair. It never even occurred to me that she could be in danger, too."

"Well, it's not your job."

"It's not yours either," she pointed out. "Not anymore." She drew in a breath, then met his eyes. "I'm sorry to pull you into this. I know it's not like we're running around doing black ops, but I also know that there's probably some crossover. And that you left that life for a reason." She paused, then added, "And for a good reason, I think."

"Jo, about this morning—"

"No. It's okay. I'm saying thank you. In a very bad way, but it's still thank you."

"In that case, you're welcome. But you don't have to thank me. The Great Trifecta, remember? SIC?"

She laughed. "Mel Swift, Jo Irwin, and Charlie

Cooper. We might have seemed like an odd group, but we were exactly the way we were supposed to be."

"We were indeed." That was why they'd arranged their acronym as they did—because *sic* was used in writing to show that something quoted that appeared wrong was in fact the actual, correct quotation.

"He was a good man," Jo said, her eyes welling. "He deserved better than what we had."

"Sounds like both of you did. And there's no point beating yourself up now. All you can do is move forward."

She shifted in her chair, then changed the subject. "Why didn't you ask Corveau to see the security footage? You just told me we need it."

"Because you're supposed to be a bereaved wife looking for answers."

"I am. I admit I'm angry about the way Mel was acting, and I wanted a divorce for more reasons than that, but I still love him. I always will, and—"

"I mean an answer to a suicide," he said gently. "Not a murder. And that seemed to be pushing it."

"But—"

"What if Corveau is part of it?"

"You mean a really good actor who was playing us?"

"It's possible. We press on something like security footage and that might be showing our hand."

"Would that be a bad thing?" Jo asked. "The bad guys are the ones who want us to locate this thing, remember?"

"Except they assume we know where it is. So from their perspective, we might be trying to locate them, and not just the MacGuffin."

"They're idiots if they think we won't."

He chuckled. "Possibly, but it's not as if we have a choice. Even if we didn't have to find this thing to protect both of us, I'd still want answers. Wouldn't you?"

"Hell, yes." She frowned, then asked, "Do you think he is? Involved, I mean."

"Honestly, no. But I also didn't know you and Mel were having problems, so maybe my take isn't that valid."

She said nothing, just held his eyes.

"What?"

"You knew we were having problems," she said. "Of course you did."

He sighed. "Yes, I did. Though the fact that you'd asked for a divorce really was news." He dragged his fingers through his hair. "I ignored all the signs, when instead I should have talked to you both. Tried to help."

"Why did you ignore them?"

Because I was terrified that if the two of you weren't together, that I'd want you, but I damn sure couldn't have you.

He didn't say that, though. Instead, he said, "Because I'm a shitty friend."

For a moment, she only sat there looking at him. Then she rose and came to his chair. She bent over and brushed a gentle kiss over his cheek. "No," she whispered. "You're not."

CHAPTER ELEVEN

"It's gonna depend on the system they've got," Mario says when we return to Stark Security after the Corveau meeting. This time, we're sitting across from him at his desk in the open area.

"Not me hacking in," he continues. "I can manage that even if it's local. But how long it takes, if we need a team, and how long they store records are all open questions. Plus, are they storing on tape? Digitally? Transferring over wi-fi or coax cable or, oh, you know."

I glance sideways at Red who, unlike me, does seem to know. "Can we unpack that a bit? Maybe slower? And with definitions?"

"Yeah. Sure. No prob." Mario's young, late-twenties, I'd guess, and has so much energy I'm already exhausted. "What exactly do you want me to run back over?"

"How do we know what kind of system? And what does it matter?"

"Right, gotcha. I can pull the plans and get some idea, but basically, that building is so old they might be on something ancient and, you know, *wired.*"

He says it like a curse, then pauses to run his fingers through thick brown hair tipped with bits of orange. "What I'm hoping is that the cameras talk to the network through wi-fi, because that's gonna be the easiest to hack. And then I'm hoping the files are stored on disk, without any sort of overwrite protocol."

"What's that?"

This time, Red answers. "It's what we do at the distillery. We don't need years of surveillance. We only need to be able to look back if there's an incident. So we overwrite our hard drives every ninety days."

"Exactamundo," Mario says, pointing a finger at me. "But none of that is a you problem. It's a me problem. I do my job, then I ring you up and tell you if it's good news or bad news. And if it's bad, I'll tell you how bad."

I glance at Red, who nods. "The sooner you can get started, the happier we'll be."

"Renly says you two are a priority, so I'm calling this his wedding present and pushing you guys to the top of my pile. Well, except for some shit I have running in the background about some fucking human trafficking network. Those people are the worst kinds of monsters."

"Human trafficking?"

It might be my imagination, but it sounds like Red's throat has gone raw.

"Yeah, we did some work a while back for a monarch whose daughter had gotten trafficked. Nasty business, but we got her out. Since then, we've had our fingers in a few things, working with an EU task force. The situation's depressing as shit, but it's a solid high when we get a win, you know?"

Red only nods, and I have the impression that he knows more than he'd like to.

"Anyhow, I'll ping you as soon as I have something. You're looking for a woman with dark hair hanging with Mel anywhere in the hotel."

"Right. But flag any woman you see him with."

"Will do," Mario says. "And I'll search the exterior cams, too. There's a rooftop pool and bar, both of which should have cameras, plus the valet area's probably wired. The parking structure, elevators, presumably the floors. I think we're going to luck out on this one," he adds as Red and I stand.

"Yeah?" Red asks. "Why's that?"

"Because Scott Lassiter was a prick," Mario says.

"The previous owner," I say.

"Right. He was time-sharing girls for fast

fucks in the hotel rooms, pardon my French," he adds to me. "But you gotta know he was filming every naughty thing that went on. That's currency, too."

"Blackmail," I say, and Mario taps his nose.

"You may be right," Red says. "I hope you are. And thanks."

"Not a problem. To me, a job like this is better than a drawer full of Snickers."

I manage a straight face when I say, "It looks like Ryan's still busy. Can you tell him what we talked about?"

"Not a problem. He may be a while, anyway. He's in with the new guy. Or maybe the borrowed guy. Not sure, honestly."

"Yeah, what is the deal with that?" The question comes from behind me, and I turn to see Renly standing there. "He was setting up his desk earlier. I thought I'd offer him those tickets for the *Moon Raiders* red carpet premier, and you would've thought I'd ask him to scrub my toilets."

"You still get free tickets?" Renly used to consult on action movies before coming full time to Stark Security.

He shrugs. "What can I say? They miss me."

"Why'd he say no?" I ask. "I'd jump all over that."

"They're yours," Renly said. "I offered them around the office, but everyone's booked. Next

Saturday. I'll be enjoying Italy from a comfy bed with a view."

"Thanks. I'll drag Red with me." I glance up, and he nods. "But I don't want to steal them out from under the new guy. He really doesn't want them?"

"His exact words were that he'd rather eat glass than walk the red carpet."

"Weird," I say. Personally, I'd be all over that.

"That's more than I got from him," Mario says. "He didn't say three words when I got his system set up."

"Ryan says he's rock solid, but keeps to himself." That from a stunning redhead who towers over me, especially as I'm still seated. "I'm Emma," she says. "You're Red—I'd recognize you even without seeing your picture on Renly's desk. You two are very much twins. And you must be Jo, the new client."

"Guilty. Well, not really."

Emma grins. "I'm sorry I missed that release party you guys had for your rye. Tony and I were grabbing a long weekend hiking in the desert."

"I'm sorry you missed it, too, but that sounds like fun."

"It was," Emma says "But what I really want is to know the details of our new recruit. More than just he doesn't like the movies. Mario? You're nerd guy. Don't tell me you haven't run his background."

Mario frowns his eyes darting to me and Red. "Paying clients, Em."

"Family," Renly retorts. "Come on, what's the deal?"

"I haven't run him," Mario says.

I almost laugh when Emma crosses her arms and cocks her head.

"Bullshit," she says.

"Okay, fuck. I tried. I failed. *Me*. Talk about a punch to the gut."

"Really?" Emma's voice rises, and she takes a step back as she says it, her attention shifting toward the glass wall of Ryan Hunter's office. I see him back there, the head of this agency, looking every bit the part. And right there with him, looking equally commanding and competent, is the tall, muscular, blond-haired god in a suit we've all been gossiping about.

I smile.

"Like him that much, do you?" Red teases.

"No," I say, though I shoot a *he really is hot* glance toward Emma. "I was just thinking that it's nice to feel included. I mean, Red's in with you guys by default, but—"

"You are, too," Red says firmly. "Isn't that right?" His eyes are hard on his brother.

"Hell, yes," Renly says.

"Yes, of course. You're one of us," Emma says.

"But spill, Mario. His file is really sealed that tight?"

"I didn't try for that long—oh, *hell*, yes I did. Couldn't find a damn thing. All I know is what Ryan gave me to put in his personnel file. His name's Simon Barré, he was born in France to a French mother and American dad, lived there until he was seventeen, then moved here. He's working on the trafficking detail, on loan from Devlin Saint. And that last part," he adds with a look to both me and Red, "really is confidential."

"The philanthropist?" I remember there was some big scandal about him not too long ago, but I don't recall the details. "His foundation helps victims of trafficking, right?"

Red closes his hand over mine. "I think Saint does a lot more than philanthropy."

"What do you know about Saint?" Mario asks.

"My brother was with the SOC," Renly says. "You know that. He could tell you, but then he'd have to kill you."

"Forget Saint," Emma says. "I want to know about Red's time with the SOC. Seagrave talks about you a lot, you know."

"You know Colonel Seagrave?"

"Who's that?" I ask.

"He's the head honcho there," Emma says. "My former boss, mentor. Practically father. As far as I'm concerned, he's one of the best people on the planet. He told me a bit about you. About how you got those scars," she adds, with a nod to Red's forearms.

"Did he?"

It may be my imagination, but Red's voice has gone cold.

"One of these days, I'd like to learn more about that. Might be something I want to look into."

She must mean following up on mission specs, but I don't understand what she means. I really want to ask, but Red says curtly, "Not something I talk much about."

"No, I suppose not. No worries. What I really want is the story on *this* guy," she says, neatly changing the subject by turning her attention to Mario as she points to Simon. "Come on, give it up, Mario. The real story. Not where he lived when he was in diapers."

"That's my point," Mario says, though I'm barely listening. Instead, I'm watching Red and noting his troubled expression. "I can't find shit," Mario complains.

"Bottom line is he doesn't play well with others," Emma says. "But I guess he's got skills that Stark and Ryan want."

Renly snorts. "You don't play well with others, either, Em. Or you didn't when you first got here. I've heard all the stories."

She spreads her arms. "Yeah, but I'm a special snowflake."

I bite back a laugh, not even thinking when I reach for Red's hand. He takes it, and I glance over at him, sharing a smile.

Later, after we get Mario's promise to call as soon as he's got something, I turn to Red in the car. "You fit in there, you know. It's already like you're one of the team."

"I wouldn't go that far. But they're good people."

"Why aren't you with them?" I press. "I know Mr. Stark tried to recruit you."

"I told you when I came home seven years ago," he says with a shrug. "I'm retired."

"Maybe you shouldn't be."

"Yes. I should." He turns to look at me, his expression hard. A few small scars mark his face, seeming to define his strong cheekbones, and I'm sure each one is the souvenir of a job. "Jo, just drop it."

His voice is low and flat and final, and as soon as he's said his piece, he turns back to concentrate on the road. I want to argue, but with what? It's not as if I have any say in what he does with his life. But the truth is, I do wonder what happened to him over there. And how much of it he brought home with him.

My attention shifts to his forearms. His Swift

Red tee has short sleeves, and there's no missing the horrible raised scars, each about five inches long and an inch wide on the outside of both forearms. I've heard a few people ask about them. Customers in the tasting room making conversation, and he always tells them the same thing: that he was in Special Forces.

For most folks, that's answer enough. For the ones who press, he says he's not at liberty to say.

Today, though, he was talking to someone who would understand, and still he brushed it off. Moreover, Emma had suggested that he got them on a mission, but I don't actually believe that's true. He was a badass in the military, sure, but the mission story just doesn't ring true.

Maybe I'm nosy or maybe I'm emboldened by the camaraderie at Stark Security. Or maybe I simply want to feel closer to this man. I don't know. But for some reason, I ask him.

For some reason, I'm stupid enough to think that maybe he'll tell me the truth.

"How did you really get those scars?"

I see his hands tighten on the steering wheel, but he doesn't turn to look at me when he says, "Jesus, Jo. Is there a reason you're interrogating me?"

"We're just talking, Red. Since when can't you talk to me?"

He exhales, and only when I'm certain he's

going to completely ignore me does he say, "I already told you. A mission."

It's true; that's what he told me. But I don't believe him. "You didn't have them when you came home," I say. "Then you went to Texas to visit your mom for six weeks, and when you came home again, you had scars. Looked like they were pretty well-healed by then, too, so whatever happened was not long after you went away. Or are you saying you went on a mission instead of back home?"

I wait for him to lie to me, because I know he went to Texas. Either that, or he'd pulled his mom into the lie, too. Because I'd texted her one day, and she'd told me that he was sleeping, doped up after a medical procedure and she was playing nurse.

"Jo..." I hear the warning in his voice, but I don't stop.

"We used to tell each other everything. Why won't you tell me about it?"

"I did. I told you they're the result of a particularly bad mission."

"So you got called back in even though you'd officially left? Or was this a Texas mission code named Medical Procedure?"

"Jo, let's drop this. We have other things to think about."

"Not until we hear back from Mario, we don't. Unless you've had some brilliant idea, we're stuck in waiting mode. And it's getting late. We should order Thai and talk. We haven't really talked in a long time."

"We can watch a movie. We can eat. We can even talk. But not about my scars. Not about my missions." He turns to me without slowing the car. "Are we clear?"

I nod, because what choice do I have?

He goes back to driving, and we make the rest of the trip in silence.

I tell myself he's right. It's none of my business. But as we continue to drive in silence, I can't deny that I truly want it to be.

CHAPTER TWELVE

A fter jumping between streaming services for what felt like a decade, we finally decided on a classic marathon. We ended up drinking wine for me and fizzy water for him and eating cheese cubes while we watched *Raiders of the Lost Ark* followed by *Back to the Future.*

As far as I'm concerned, it was about as perfect as an evening can get.

It's the *after* part that's hard. This uncomfortable moment in which I find myself alone in my room with only my thoughts to keep me company. Dark thoughts about mysterious packages and my husband slipping slowly beneath the fermenting mash.

Well, shit.

For over an hour, I beg sleep to spirit me away, but to no avail, so I once again slide out of bed, then head to the guest bedroom. Although to be honest, it's only been a guest bedroom since last night when Red slept there. For most of the last year, it had been Mel's room. When he'd stayed at home, anyway.

Then again, all things considered, maybe it was a guest room even then.

I hesitate at the door, remembering Red's reaction this morning, and I almost turn back. But I don't. I stay.

I tell myself it's only because I don't want to be alone, but that's a lie. The truth is that I don't want to be alone knowing that Red is right there, just a few feet away in a room separated from mine by nothing more substantial than the guest bathroom.

What I want is him.

Not sexually—or, at least, I tell myself that's not what I want—but simply the comfort of knowing that even though the world has turned upside down, he's still here for me.

And that's why I gently push open his door, then give it a quick tap. It wouldn't be enough to wake me, but I know Red's a light sleeper, and I see his eyes flicker in the ambient light.

"Can I sleep here?"

One eye opens, his expression bordering on a scowl. "Do you remember this morning? I don't think it's a good idea."

I sigh as I lean against the doorjamb, only then

noticing Romeo curled up in the armchair in the corner of the room. I smile, but my attention turns back to Red. "I wish you'd tell me why."

He closes his eyes and is silent for so long, I start to think he's fallen back asleep. "You're right. We haven't talked much. Not like before."

I take a step forward, not sure if that's an invitation or not, but willing to be bold. "We used to talk all the time. I'd tell you every stupid thought in my head. I even told you about the fiasco when I slept with—oh, God. I don't even remember his name."

"Timothy Brant."

"You remember that?"

His eyes open slowly, and he watches as I continue to cross the room, then sit on the edge of the bed, just inches from his hips. I wait for him to tell me to go back to my room, but he surprises me by pushing himself up, then settling his back against the padded headboard. "I remember a lot of things. That weekend you lived at the kitchen table while you wrote that paper on—what was it?"

"Oh, man." I let my head flop back as I groan. "Why are you torturing me? I hated that class. It sounded so cool in the catalog, but that stupid paper killed it for me. The relevance and meaning of sun imagery in Nordic mythology. I mean, ugh. Before I wrote it, I loved mythology. Now I cringe every time I watch an Avengers movie with Thor in it."

He chuckles. "I learned a few new curse words that weekend."

I tilt my head. "I do *not* believe that. But I do remember how sweet you and Mel were. You had your own classwork, but you still fetched me fast food and made me gallons of coffee. And the cake," I add. "The cake was the best."

I'd returned home after turning in the accursed paper to find a chocolate frosted sheet cake with *You did it!* spelled out in messy icing letters.

"The cake was easy, except for the fact that we had no eggs in the apartment. The writing was hard."

"It was fabulous. One of my best memories." We'd spent the evening drinking and playing Never Have I Ever, and sharing far too many secrets, most of which I don't remember.

"Oh, I remember some," he says, when I tell him as much.

I cringe. "Please tell me that's not true."

"That was the night we learned that you'd never been on the giving end of oral sex."

I let my face fall into my hands. "I have no memory of saying that."

"But you did. Do you remember what I told you?"

I look up, because now that he's asked, I actually do remember it. "You teased the shit out of me and offered to let me practice on you. Mel was cracking up. He said he'd be willing to tape it if I tried. For instructional comment and critique. You jerks."

"You were cracking up, too," he says. "So was I, for that matter. I laughed so hard my sides hurt."

"I miss those days," I say softly.

He rubs the pad of his thumb lightly over my knee, exposed in the sleep shorts and tank I'm wearing. "True confessions?" I almost don't hear him, his voice is so low.

"Sure." My voice is breathy, and I'm not sure why. Something in his tone. Something signaling a change.

"I meant it. That night. That offer. I can't tell you how much I wanted you to take me up on it."

I swallow, then force a light-hearted giggle. "No way do I believe that."

"Oh, yes. Hell, Jo. I've wanted you since the day I met you."

"I—" I suck in a breath, suddenly far too aware of his touch. "Why didn't you say something in college? And that night after you came back from overseas—the night we kissed—why did you pull away? For that matter, why didn't you say something when I asked if you were okay with me dating Mel?"

I think I hear regret in his sigh. "What does it matter now?"

"No," I snap. "You're the one who opened this

door. And you're the one touching me right now. Do you even know what you're doing to me, with just that stupid touch of your thumb? All the things you're making me want?"

He doesn't move his thumb, but he does meet my eyes before purposefully dropping his gaze. I know what he sees. My nipples are hard against my tank. And if he'd just slide that hand higher, he'll find out that I'm wet. *Please, please, just a little bit higher.*

But he doesn't budge. Instead he takes a deep breath, then starts speaking, his voice low, his eyes rising to meet mine. Worst of all, he pulls his hand away, stealing his touch.

"Before I joined the service, I was too stupid to say anything to you. And I told myself a fairy tale. That nothing would change while I was gone, and when I came back, I'd have the courage to say something. Like I was some storybook hero who had to go away to prove his worth."

"You're back now," I whisper, but even as I say the words, I know he's not finished with the story. Because he came back years ago. And despite that fairy tale he's espousing, he didn't claim me that night, back when it was only him and me, and Mel was just a friend.

Instead, he very firmly pushed me away.

"Things changed, Jo."

I swallow rising tears, but manage a nod.

"I've always wanted you. But I can't have you."

"Why not? I'm here, aren't I? *What* changed?"

He draws in a deep breath. "I won't tell you that."

I feel the tears spill down my cheeks as I put the pieces together. "The scars," I whisper. "The ones on your arms. Did you try to kill yourself?" They're not in the right place, but what else could they be?

He scoffs. "No. That was the one thing I never did. Maybe I should have."

My palm lands hard against his cheek before I even realize I'm going to slap him.

"I'm sorry," he says, and I know we're both thinking of Mel. It wasn't suicide. But for those long, horrible hours, I'd believed that it was.

"That was a stupid thing to say," I snap.

"I know. I'm truly sorry."

I draw in a breath, then let it out slowly. "It was that bad?"

"It was that bad." He holds out his arms, indicates the scars with his chin. "These aren't from trying to kill myself. They're to save myself."

"I don't understand."

"A reminder."

"Of what?"

His face goes blank and for a moment, I think he's slipped inside himself. Then he says, "That there are ways to cope."

I shake my head. "You're not making sense."

The corner of his mouth twitches, and I see a hint of humor in his eyes. "I'm not trying to."

I scowl, then exhale. "Thanks. I mean that, by the way. It's not my attempt at sarcasm."

"I'm glad to hear that. But what are you thanking me for?"

"For opening up to me. Not a lot," I add, when his eyes widen in surprise. "But a smidgeon."

"Hmm." He shifts on the bed, leaning toward me. "Do you promise not to ask me more questions tonight?"

"What if I say yes?"

He reaches over and folds down the covers on the other side of the bed.

"You're sure?"

"Just sleep. Just so we're clear."

"I get it."

I move to the other side of the bed, then slide in. He moves down until he's flat, then rolls over, his back to me. "Goodnight, Jo," he says.

"Night, Red."

I watch him breathe in the dim light, the way his back moves. The way the tats on his arm—an abstract pattern of mostly reds and blacks that match his chest—seem to pop in the light as if they're portents of a coming storm.

I let them lead me toward sleep, and I'm on the

verge of drifting off when I realize something. "Red," I say. "Red, we're idiots."

"I never doubted it." His reply is so soft and mumbled I barely make it out.

"I mean it. We were right there at the hotel."

"What?" He rolls over to face me.

"You said it yourself. Hotels have safe deposit boxes. Some do anyway."

At first, he looks baffled. Then I see the remnants of sleep clear, replaced by a smile. He bends forward and presses a soft kiss to my forehead.

"And now we have a plan for tomorrow," he says.

CHAPTER THIRTEEN

"This has to be it," Jo said as they left Red's hybrid with The Terrace Hotel's valet. "He had something to protect, apparently he came here all the time, so of course he'd lock it up here. It's elementary, my dear Mr. Cooper."

Red chuckled, glancing sideways at her. "You're in a good mood."

She lifted her shoulders. "I feel like we're finally on to something. There's going to be something here. You know I'm right."

"It's a good bet, I won't deny that."

She hipchecked him as they stepped into the lobby. "That's not optimism. That's a lack of pessimism."

"I'm going to go with pragmatism."

"Fair enough. Of our dynamic duo, I'll be the one with vision. You can be the one who slogs."

"Seems like a fair trade to me."

"That's not the only thing supporting my good mood," she added.

"No?" They retraced their steps from yesterday across the gilded lobby to the registration desk. "Dare I ask?"

"It's because of you. Us. Last night."

He cocked his head. She'd been angling for sex, which he'd firmly shut down. So unless he'd done more than talk in his sleep...

"I can *so* read your mind, pervo, and no we didn't, but it would serve you right if we had."

He laughed, not surprised at all that she really could read his mind. "If it wasn't mind-blowing sex, then tell me what life transformative thing happened last night that I missed?"

They'd reached the counter. "We talked," she said, her smile as bright as sunshine. "I was afraid we'd lost that, but we haven't. And that, Mr. Pragmatist, makes me happy."

She turned away to signal the clerk, leaving him reeling a bit. He wasn't sure what he'd expected, but this ... well, she was right. They'd talked more last night than they had in years. He'd feared they'd lost that connection, too, but clearly they hadn't.

Despite this hellish situation they were trying to navigate, they'd found the core of their friendship again, and that truly was incredible.

The only thing better, in fact, would be to take that friendship to the next level, but as he'd told her last night, that would never—could never—happen. So all he said as the clerk approached was, "Yeah. That makes me happy, too."

He moved closer to the counter, his arm brushing hers. As if in contradiction to his thoughts, the contact sent sparks of awareness shooting through him, forcing him to stifle a groan.

Shut it down, Red. You know it's not happening, so just shut it the fuck down.

"You're certain?"

Red glanced up, realized Jo was talking to the clerk, and kicked himself for being so off his game that he'd actually tuned their conversation out.

"You don't even do short term boxes for hotel guests?"

"No, ma'am," the clerk said. "The rooms all have safes. I've been here since Mr. Corveau took over the property. As far as I know, this hotel never had deposit boxes."

"I was so sure," Jo said later when they were back in Red's car. "It just made sense, you know?"

"Nothing about this makes sense." He muttered a soft curse, as disappointed as she was that their potential lead crapped out.

"So what now?"

"I don't know."

Her eyes were wide as she looked at him. "We

have to figure it out." There was a hint of panic in her voice. "It's not going to just go away."

"No," Red said, his hands tightening on the steering wheel. "And the longer it takes, the more insistent they'll become."

"By insistent, you mean violent. Like that's going to suddenly make us remember that we know what the hell this stupid package is, and where Mel stashed it?"

The panic had morphed into fear and fury, but he didn't try to calm her down or argue. She was right on all counts.

"We need to swing by my place," he said, focusing on the pragmatic side of planning since he had nothing else up his sleeve. "I'm staying with you until this is sorted out, and I need to get a few things."

He glanced sideways at her, expecting an argument, but she only nodded.

He took the next left, mentally rerouting them toward his mid-Wilshire condo rather than her house in the valley. The condo was old enough that it didn't have parking, and he reached into the middle console for his resident parking pass, which he slid onto the dashboard.

He started looking for spaces on either side of the street once he was within a few blocks. Almost all the slots were full, some clearly not by residents. Like the dark car with tinted windows and no resident tag. He frowned, making a mental note as a bona fide miracle occurred, and a spot opened up right in front of his building.

"It's our lucky day," he told her.

She made a sour face. "If a parking space meets your standards, we really need to have a talk about what our goals here are." But she was grinning as he reached her side of the car.

Before they started walking toward his building, he took a moment to survey his perimeter—a habit he'd acquired over the years, and not one he ever intended to break.

He frowned, considering that.

She tilted her head, studying him. "What's wrong?"

"Not sure. I was thinking about Monday. I told you that someone nailed me with a Taser."

She cringed, but nodded. "And?"

"They shouldn't have been able to."

"Well, duh. You're Bad Ass Secret Agent Guy."

"I'm serious. I always check my surroundings. It's ingrained. I don't think I could stop if I wanted to."

She paused on the steps leading up to the main entrance. "What are you getting at?"

He took her arm and led her inside, then stopped in the entryway.

"These aren't your average thugs we're dealing

with," he said, his voice low. "Whoever they are, they're pros."

"I figured as much. I mean, think about the way they killed Mel." She swallowed, clearly fighting a shudder. "And then the video. Maybe Mel got hooked up with, I don't know, the mafia or something. Maybe they wanted him to launder money."

"No, you're not understanding me. I don't mean professional criminals. I mean they're operatives. They're like me—like I was, anyway. Probably retired. Definitely skilled."

"Oh." The word was small, but she followed it with a forced smile. "So I guess we're living in an action movie."

He made a rough noise in his throat. "And despite turning down Stark's offer, it looks like I'm back in that goddamn life. At least for a little while."

She reached over and took his hand. "I'm really sorry," she said. "But, Red, I can't tell you how glad I am that I'm not going through this alone."

His heart twisted, and he wanted to give himself a hard, solid punch to the head. What the hell was he doing telling her all that? Scaring her more than she already was?

"Do not even," she said as they stepped into the elevator to go to his ninth floor unit.

"Don't what?" he asked as the elevator started to rise.

"Regret telling me the truth about what we're in the middle of."

"Stop reading my mind."

She shrugged and flashed him a lighthearted grin. "It's what I do."

God, how he wanted to kiss her right then.

"What?" she said, her eyes narrowing as she studied his face.

He dodged with another truth. "Everything we're in the middle of, and you can still laugh."

"Oh." She looked down, and he watched as her shoulders rose and fell, and he wanted to kick himself.

"Jo, hey, I didn't mean that as a bad—"

"I know you didn't." She met his eyes, hers hard with determination. "I'm not naive, Red. I know the depth of mire we're in. But I can't wallow in it. That wouldn't do anyone any good. And yes, I miss Mel—I do. It pisses me off that I can't even mourn him properly."

The elevator car came to a stop and the doors opened, but she didn't make a move. "I hate that he died when our marriage was in trouble," she continued. "And I hate the fact that no matter what was going on between us, the real tragedy is that I lost a friend. Both of us lost a friend."

She took a deep breath, then pressed the button to keep the elevator doors open, even though she didn't budge from the small car. "But I can't be that person. I don't want to be. So I choose to look at the good side."

"The good side," he repeated.

"Yeah," she said, finally stepping off the elevator.

"And what's that?"

She glanced over his shoulder with a *well, duh* look. "*You*, dummy."

"I'm not sure I'm qualified to be anybody's good side," he said, following her to his unit.

"I'm not going through this alone, which is a bonus. We've been rebuilding a friendship, which we both know had started to flounder."

"No. We were—"

"I don't mean like that. We'll be friends forever. But like we talked about last night. It wasn't as ... I don't know ... *intimate* as it had been before. And now I feel like we're back. That's all."

She stepped aside to let him get his key into the door, and he was grateful for the diversion. Otherwise she might have seen the evidence of the way that word—*intimate*—had shot through him, firing all sorts of lust-filled responses that had no business firing.

"I get it," he said, pushing the door open. He hurried inside. "I'm going to go pack a bag," he said, then he was off, leaving her to make herself at home while he took a breather in the back.

Because damn it, this had to stop. He couldn't

keep thinking about her like that. Couldn't keep
wanting her. Craving her.

But he did. He always had.

And how much of an asshole did it make him
that all these feelings had bubbled to the surface in
the wake of his buddy's death. "God, Mel, I'm
sorry. I'm so fucking sorry."

Behind him, Jo cleared her throat. "I didn't
mean to interrupt—I only wanted to know if you
wanted me to pack up your plants on the patio and
bring them along. I mean, if you're staying until this
is over, it may be awhile."

He shook his head. "My neighbor has a key. I'll
ask her to check in on them."

"Oh."

He frowned, confused by the hard tone of her
voice.

"Are you guys dating? Because you should
explain to her why you're coming to stay with
me if—"

"I told you. I don't date."

"She has a key. Is she one of the ones you—"

"Christ, Jo. She's my neighbor. She's eighty-
two, and although I think she's one of the best
people I've ever met, I can't quite see her in that
role."

"Right." She drew in a breath. "I'm sorry. It's
just on my mind."

He blinked at her. "What is?"

"Well, duh. You. Me. Sex."

He stumbled backwards, then sat on the edge of the bed.

She kept talking, not seeming to care at all that she'd just tossed him a curve ball. "You said no, and I respect that. But dammit, Red, it's on my mind."

"Sex?" What the hell was happening?

"Hello? Yes. And God knows I shouldn't be thinking along those lines, at all. Not with Mel gone like that and people attacking us. But I am." She'd been pacing, but now she paused in front of him.

"I'd say it's that I want comfort," she continued. "You know, after Mel. After everything. And I think that's part of it. Mostly, though, I want a taste of what we never had. What we should have had that night you pushed me away."

"How can you do that?" he asked, utterly fascinated by her. "How can you lay it all out there like that? I've never known anyone that comfortable with honesty."

Her cheeks turned pink, and he watched as her throat moved. "Yeah, well, maybe this is the new me. I wasn't honest enough with Mel. About wanting to try harder when it started to go downhill, or about wanting a clean break when I was certain it wasn't working anymore. You're meeting the new Jo, I guess."

"No. Same Jo. Just a new perspective."

"At any rate, I hope you like Jo-two-point-oh."

He reached for her hand as he stood up. "You know I do. Just like you know this thing between us isn't going anywhere."

She bit her lower lip and moved closer. "So you admit there's a thing."

"I never denied the thing."

"But you really won't tell me what's holding you back?" She moved closer still, then slid her hands around his waist, her body pressed to his. "Even if I beg?"

He stifled a groan, trying to halt his body's reaction, his traitorous cock that wanted to join in these games she was playing. And she knew exactly what she was doing, too. Of that he was certain. There was no way she could miss the erection straining against his jeans, not when her body was pressed flat against his.

He drew in a breath, caught that scent of strawberries from her hair, and just about lost control. Instead, he used the rising need as a lever, giving him the will to spin them around so that he could push her back, tumbling her onto the bed.

She gasped, a soft, startled sound, and he was on her in an instant, straddling her, his hands on her shoulders, holding her down.

"Yes," she whispered.

"No," he said. "I know you're just playing. I

know you don't understand. But you have to believe me. This is a door you don't want to open."

"I'm not playing."

He managed a derisive snort. "There really are monsters in the dark, Jo. And I promise, if you push too hard, you'll meet the ones that live in me."

She licked her lips, but she didn't look scared. On the contrary, when she parted those moist lips, all she said was, "Let me."

And that's when he realized the truth: Between the two of them, she was the one with no fear. While he was fucking terrified.

CHAPTER FOURTEEN

"Wait a second," Red says, his hand going out to stop me before I continue down the steps. We're in front of the entrance to the condo, looking out toward the tree-lined street.

"What's going on?"

"That car. The black one with the tinted windows."

I see the car he's talking about, but nothing stands out to me. "What about it?"

He doesn't say. Instead he takes a step forward, then glances back at me. "Stay here."

He doesn't wait for me to respond, just continues down the walk until he reaches the curb. He pauses, then takes a step into the street, between two parked cars. Traffic is light, but there are enough cars that he can't cross immediately.

As he hesitates, I notice that the car in question

is starting to pull out. Traffic clears enough for him to start to cross, and as he does, the car guns its engine, then screeches away.

I hurry down the sidewalk toward the curb as Red continues crossing, then seems to inspect the area where the car was only moment before.

I watch all of this, baffled, until he comes back to me.

"What is it?"

"Surveillance. On us."

My eyes go wide. "Are you serious?"

"As a heart attack."

"How can you be so sure?" I don't actually doubt him. The car definitely seemed to be zipping away from Red specifically. "And why did you notice that car in the first place?"

"Instinct."

"Okay, but *why*?"

"No resident tag. And there was someone sitting in the passenger seat, not the driver's side."

"Maybe they were waiting for someone. And how do you know that anyway? The windows were tinted."

"The windshield isn't."

"Yeah, but from our angle at the condo, we couldn't see the windshield," I tell him.

"I didn't see it when we came out, I saw it when we pulled in."

"You're telling me that as we pulled in on our

side of the street, you just happened to notice some-body sitting in the passenger side in a car across the street?"

He just shrugs.

"And that was it?"

"When we came out, the back window was cracked. The front window was cracked when we first arrived."

"Well, I'm seriously impressed. And that's not instinct."

"No?"

"No," I insist. "It's training. And skill. And honestly it's pretty creepy that someone was just sitting there watching your place for who knows how long, but it's seriously impressive that you tagged them. Is that the word?"

He shrugs. "It's a word. It works."

I laugh. "Well, whatever the word, I can tell you that I feel better having you beside me."

The words weren't intended in any sort of sexual sense, but as soon as they're out of my mouth, I realize that's how I mean them. I *do* want him beside me, and not only standing next to me, protecting me from bad guys.

I want him *beside* me. In my life, in my bed. I want *him*. Charlie Cooper.

But I've already told him most of that, and it didn't get me anywhere. So for now at least, I push those feelings aside. It's not like I have nothing else occupying my mind. I'm full up on interesting topics. Like, oh, coming up with a plan for staying alive, avoiding the bad guys, and finding the damn MacGuffin.

Just another day in LA.

I exhale, frustrated and tired. "Why do you think they're watching us?"

He starts to walk toward his car, his hand lightly at my back. "I assume they're making sure that we're really looking for this thing."

He clicks the button on his fob and unlocks the car, then opens my door for me.

"Hello?" I say as I slide into the passenger seat. "They've attacked both of us, and they killed Mel. Hell yeah, I'm looking for it."

I look up at him, still standing there with the door in his hand. "That won't be the end of it will it?" I ask. "I mean, once we find this thing, it's not over, is it?"

His shoulders rise and fall as he shuts the door. I watch as he circles the front of the car and then enters. "That won't be the end, will it?" I repeat, the words heavy on my tongue.

"It would be nice if it was."

I exhale, not liking the answer. Because we both know damn well that once they have the missing thing back, there's no reason to keep us alive. We'll have become a liability.

"So what do we do?" I ask as he pulls into traffic.

"What we've been doing. We find this thing. Then we'll have leverage, and we go from there."

"You know what I said earlier about having you beside me?"

He glances toward me—a quick glance since he's driving, but I swear I see the heat in his eyes. Right now, though, I don't care.

Right now, that's not what I'm thinking about at all. "It goes double now."

I settle back in my seat, wishing I had a coffee. I could use the caffeine hit right about now. I'm about to ask for him to find a drive-thru, when the sound of his ringing phone reverberates through the car.

The in-dash screen identifies the caller as Ryan, and Red taps the button to accept the call. "What's up?"

Immediately, Ryan's voice fills the car. "You driving?"

"Yeah. Do you need us to come there?"

"Find a place where you can pull over. I've got something I want you to take a look at. I'm going to send it to your phone."

"I have my tablet in my bag," I say. "Send it there and we'll be able to see it better." I give him my number so he can text it, and as he sends the image and I open the file, Red pulls into a nearby parking lot to pull over.

"Tell me when you've got it open," Ryan says. "And by the way, the phones are done. Mario popped by your place to deliver yours, but since you weren't there, he let himself in. I apologize. Mario sometimes forgets the smaller things like, oh, privacy, in the bigger picture."

I laugh. "It's all good. Tell him thanks."

"He's here with me. And what I told him was to ask permission first next time, and that you'll report in if you see anything odd. We'll look at the other clone in the meantime."

"Sorry about that," Mario says. "Figured you'd want it right away."

"Not a problem," I say, and I can practically hear Ryan rolling his eyes.

"The picture loaded," I add. "Signal's not great here. Is it supposed to be this grainy?"

"That's the best we've got. The system wasn't hi-res by a long shot."

I have my tablet balanced between Red and me on the console. We're looking at two people in a hallway. Mel's looking over his shoulder, his arm around a woman with long, dark hair facing away from the camera. My stomach clenches at their intimate pose, but I try to analyze the photo, not my irritation that he had a sidepiece.

"Dammit, Mel," I whisper. "If you were

fucking her, why the hell didn't you just sign the divorce papers?"

Red reaches over and takes my hand. "Can you clean it up?" he says to Ryan.

"It's doubtful, but I'm trying," Mario says.

"Is that a mirror in the hall?" Red asks. I look more closely and see what he's referring to. There's something there, visible in the gap between their heads. It's round, and has something blurry in the middle of it.

"You got it," Mario says. "But that's as clean as I've gotten the reflection. If we can get it, we'll have our girl. But I gotta tell you, confidence is low."

"So what's the plan?" I ask.

"If we found this, we can probably find more," Mario says. "I'm all over it. This and the exterior cameras. More light. Might get a better quality image. Bottom line, I'm on it."

Once we end the call, Red pulls back out onto the road. For a while we drive in silence, and I wonder what he's thinking. Mel was my husband, but I wouldn't have expected him to tell me about an affair, though it would've been nice if he'd agreed to the divorce. But he was Red's best friend, and unless Red was lying to me, he didn't have a clue about the affair either.

I've been nursing my wounds, but in that moment I realize that Red suffered the same kind of betrayal I did. With a friendship that close, why didn't Mel turn to him? Why didn't he tell him that our marriage was in trouble? That he was seeing someone else?

These are all questions I know I'll never have the answer to, and it eats at me, but at the very least, I'm grateful that I'm not going through this alone.

We're over the hill and in Studio City when another thought occurs to me. "What if she's not in danger?" I ask. "What if he was having an affair with someone who was actually plotting to kill him?"

"Not a bad theory, but it raises the question of why she'd want to kill someone like Mel. Was he into something shady? Did she pull him in?" He looks sideways at me. "Would that make you feel better? If his mistress was his killer?"

I sit up straighter, shocked by the question. "Like that's what he deserves because he screwed around? God, no. I just wish I knew why he didn't agree to a divorce."

"Mel was never good at admitting he was wrong," Red says. "Maybe he didn't want to face the truth."

I sit for a moment, watching the familiar buildings go by. "Maybe. I guess I get that. It's hard to own up to who you are sometimes. To get out of your own way."

The words linger in the air, and I have to wonder how much they apply to Red. There's something between us. I know it. I felt it. Good God, I've felt it since the first day I met the man. And now, in the midst of all this tragedy, he's even admitted it to me. And yet he's not willing to do a damn thing about it. Is he not willing to get out of his own way either?

With a sigh, I lean back and close my eyes, wishing that everything were different. But it's not, and this is the new normal, and we're going to get through this. I have to believe that, because the only other option is that we don't find this thing, and my world crumbles even more. Possibly all the way into dust and ash.

"Is your mom coming for the wedding?" I blurt the words out in an attempt to get my mind off the subject.

He laughs. "Is that a subtle way to change the subject?" I roll my eyes at how well he knows me.

"I didn't think it was subtle at all."

He chuckles. "No, she's not coming. She planned to, but Elise fell and broke her hip, so they can't travel."

"Oh, I didn't know. Will she be okay?"

"Yeah, Mom says it's healing well. She'll have to be careful with it, but she's doing okay."

"Good. I like Elise. She was a hoot that one time they came to visit when we were in college, and we went to the Getty with them. Do you remember?"

"I do. That was a good day."

Elise, who at one point taught art history, had been our private tour guide. But she made it so much fun, telling us stories about the pieces that she knew something about, and making up things if she didn't. It was the only time I've ever wandered through a museum and alternated between learning something and laughing my ass off.

I adored her from that moment on, and I was truly happy when I learned that Red's mom and Elise, who I'd always thought were just longtime besties, had recently gotten married.

"I'm sad they aren't coming," I say. "I'd love to see them both again, and I was really hoping to practice on your mom."

"You've been practicing sign language?" I hear real surprise in his voice.

"A little. I'm trying to not forget the basics, then expand a bit beyond that."

We're at a light, and he turns to look at me, a question in his eye. "Why?"

I can only shrug. The real answer is because it was important to him. What I say is, "I want to learn it. I've been practicing since college, you know that." I'm not good, but I can communicate. Sort of. I'm like a first-year French student in a

Paris tourist restaurant where the staff speaks perfect English.

Red keeps his gaze on me for a little bit longer than necessary, so long that the person behind us honks when the light turns green. As he accelerates, I ask my other question.

"Is your dad coming?"

"He's not invited. If it were a typical wedding, he might be invited to the ceremony, but it's just going to be Renly and Abby. And Renly isn't interested in having him at the party afterwards."

"Right. I forgot." Red and his father have a decent relationship now, but their dad walked out on them when they were kids, and it made for some rocky times. Red patched it up with his dad, but not Renly. And then, when Renly joined the service right out of high school despite his father telling him it was a horrible idea, it drove that wedge deeper.

"Renly didn't like being told what to do, especially by a man who'd proved he didn't much care about us when he walked away. And Dad doesn't like being ignored. They can be civil now, but ... well, I can't blame my brother. Dad was absent for most of our lives."

"You repaired the relationship."

"True, but I reached out on purpose. It was my choice. Not reaching out is Renly's."

"I get that. But I'm glad that you did. And

envious too. It's hard for me not to criticize Renly's choices, you know?"

He reaches over and squeezes my hand, knowing full well that I've always been a bit jealous that his absentee father at least kept in touch, even sporadically. And his mom's still alive. "You've got a different perspective. But everyone does. It would be pretty boring if we were all the same."

I manage a smile to push away the melancholy. "Yeah. It really would."

When we arrive at my place, Red parks in the driveway behind my car. We get to the front door, and see that among everything else, Mario has installed a shiny new lock.

I'm punching in the code when my phone rings. I pull it out, glance at it, and almost drop my phone. Red catches it as it starts to tumble from my fingers. He looks at me in shock, obviously having seen the same thing on the screen as I did—the call is from Mel's office number.

I meet his eyes, then tap the speaker button to answer the call.

"You need to work harder," an electronically altered voice says. "Think harder. Otherwise we may decide we don't need your help at all."

I see a red dot appear on the door in front of me. For a moment I'm confused, then the dot moves to me. My mouth goes dry and my pulse pounds in my ears as I look down and see the dot on my white tee.

Suddenly I'm slammed backwards, and Red is in front of me, his body crushing mine against the side of the house, blocking me. Protecting me. "You know damn well I'm the one with the best chance of finding this thing," Red says, still talking to the speakerphone. "You hurt her, you lose me."

"I don't believe that, Mr. Cooper. But if you work faster, then maybe we won't have to see which one of us is right."

I can't see anything from behind Red, so I don't know if the laser dot is gone. We stay that way for a moment, completely still, until Red finally moves forward, giving me room to breathe.

He turns and punches in my code, so hard I'm surprised the little numbers don't crush into dust. I can see the rage boiling inside him; it's practically coming off in waves.

He takes my hand, pulling me so that I stumble inside, surprised by the urgency since the threat is gone. He follows me, slams the door, and the next thing I know my back is flat against the closed door, and his mouth is hard against mine.

I'm melting. Completely melting, and I want this so much. I want to work away the fear, the loss the anger. I want everything he's giving, and I want to give everything he's taking.

He's touching my face, his calloused fingertips

rough on my skin. His eyes meet mine, then trail over my entire body as if he can't believe I'm here. I gasp, his intense inspection like the most intimate of caresses.

"Red," I begin, but he cuts me off with a kiss so deep I feel it all through my body. His hand goes to my neck, holding me in place so tight I can barely breathe. Then his other hand slides down inside my leggings to cup my bare sex, and I almost come right then.

I'm already so wet, and I moan as he thrusts his fingers inside me, hard and deep, his kiss mimicking the way he's finger-fucking me. I'm trapped, immobile, needy, and desperate for more.

I try to shift my hips, so desperate for his touch, wanting—*needing*—to grind against his hand. Needing that release. But I'm trapped, completely at his mercy. It's heady and glorious, and all I want is more.

Then suddenly, the cage is gone. He's stepped away, his hands and mouth no longer touching me.

Instead, he's looking at me as if he doesn't know me, and I'm so lost right now that I don't even know myself. "Red? What—"

"I'm sorry," he says, his voice an echo of pain. "Jo, I'm so fucking sorry."

CHAPTER FIFTEEN

What the hell was he doing?

Red pushed back from her, feeling like a complete subhuman when her hand went to her neck, her eyes wide, her lips parted. She was breathing hard, just staring at him. And why not? He'd trapped her, basically attacked her, and had just kept on claiming her even when she'd struggled against him.

"I'm sorry. I'm so fucking sorry." That was all he could get out. All he could say.

What words were there that would fill the void he'd just created between them? A looming black chasm that he'd never be able to cross.

God, he'd never wanted her to see him like this.

"So fucking sorry," he repeated, then bolted from the living room, slamming himself into the guest room and leaning against the door as if to barricade himself inside.

He drew in a breath, then another and another until he could see straight again. Until his heart stopped beating so hard that he risked cracking a rib. When he could get the picture of her shocked expression out of his mind.

Jo. Of all the people he didn't want to see him like this, why did he have to lose it in front of Jo?

It was rhetorical question, of course. He knew exactly why. *He wanted her.*

But his shame was that he craved her *that* way. In all the dark ways, the dark places where he lived now, he wanted her there with him, but dammit, he was never going to do that to her.

With an angry burst he pushed away from the door and started pacing. He had to deal with this. He had to bring it down. He could feel the rage and the fury and then need bubbling through him.

He was on the edge, and he had to get it out. Had to release those demons.

He had to fight back.

"Fuck it," he murmured, then reached into his back pocket and pulled out his phone. He hit the speed dial number, leaving the phone on speaker as he paced, waiting for her to answer.

"Mr. R, it's lovely to hear from you." Her voice was soft and polished. The voice of a woman you could trust.

"I need somebody," he growled.

"Right away, I assume?"

"Yes. I'll need a hotel room. Can you arrange it?"

"Of course. Just tell me what time, and—"

"What the hell are you doing?"

He whipped around to find Jo standing in the doorway. In two long strides she crossed to him and ripped the phone out of his hand.

"He'll call you back." She ended the call and tossed the phone on the bed.

He took a step toward her, certain his expression would terrify even the most hardened military man. Jo stood her ground.

"Is that her? A call girl you see? What the fuck are you thinking?"

It was a valid question. He couldn't leave Jo now even though, dammit, he'd sure as hell proved that he couldn't stay around her either.

"Dammit, Red, answer me."

"Her name is Marjorie. She runs an escort service. And yes, she was going to arrange a girl for me."

He didn't see the slap coming. He only felt it the sting on his cheek. She took a step back, breathing hard.

He stepped closer. "I'd be careful if I were you. I'm not myself right now." He shook his head. "No, that's not the truth. I am myself right now. That's the goddamn problem."

"Bullshit. I don't know what's going on with you, but I do know you're running away. You're running away from me to go pay someone to fuck you. Why?"

He could hear the hurt in her voice, and his heart twisted.

"Dammit, Jo. It's a transaction, not a relationship. I don't have to worry what they think of either me or what I need. I pay the money, I get whatever I ask. Is that what you want to hear?"

He expected her to cringe away in disgust. Instead, she tilted her head back and met his eyes, hers just as cold and hard as he was certain his were. "Yes. That's exactly what I wanted to hear."

"Well, then you've heard. And now you know." He started to push past her out of the room, but she grabbed his arm.

"Why?" Her voice was soft now, almost tentative. "Why them and not me?"

The words ricocheted through him. *Why indeed?* Because wasn't that what he really wanted? To pull her into his arms. To wrap her in his embrace. To draw her close and slowly strip her from her clothes. To trail kisses over her skin. To taste her and touch her.

Yes, dear God, yes. But he wanted so much more than that, too. Needed so much more.

Raw, hard things. He wanted—no, he needed—

to burn what was raging inside of him out of him. And he wanted it to be Jo who stoked that fire.

He would never do that to her.

Instead, he cupped her cheek and said, "I love you Jo. But you know what the song says. You can't always get what you want."

CHAPTER SIXTEEN

I didn't mean to fall asleep on the couch, but I must have, because I'm awakened when Red presses his hand to my shoulder. The room is entirely dark now, and I have no sense of time.

He sits on the edge of the sofa, his hip brushing against my torso. I stretch and curl onto my side, squishing my back against the cushions to give him more room.

"Are you okay?" I ask. He's looking at me so strangely, as if he's never seen me before.

"I'm sorry."

I wait, but he doesn't say anything else. "It's okay," I say. "I didn't have any right to interrupt or to make you feel bad or for any of it, honestly." I don't understand what he's battling, but I know it's something, and I hate the thought that I made it worse for him. "I'm the one who should be apologizing."

He's shaking his head as I talk. Now I reach out and put my hand on his knee.

"No. I mean it. I'm not in your head, but I know that whatever's there is dark. I don't understand why. But I shouldn't have burst in like that and started railing on you."

He drops his head, so I have no view of his face. But when he finally tilts it back up again and looks me in the eyes, I can see the intensity reflected there. The flashes of emotion that catch in the dim ambient light peeking in around the curtains.

I stay still and silent, waiting for him to speak. Even Rambo, curled up near my feet, hasn't moved, as if he knows that anything out of the ordinary might shift Red offtrack, might keep him from saying whatever it is he's come out here to say.

And so I wait, almost waiting until I think he's not going to say anything at all. Then I hear his voice, so low and gravelly that I almost don't recognize it. "It was almost a year," he says. "Almost a year that I was there, trapped and tortured. A hostage."

My body goes completely cold, and I have to physically tense my jaw to keep my teeth from chattering. I open my mouth, but I don't know what I'm going to say, and I'm relieved when he continues.

"I remember all of it. Not just in my mind, I remember it in my blood. I remember it in my soul. They changed me. *She* changed me. She twisted me around, and even though I won in the end, I didn't really. Because they broke me, Jo. They completely shattered me. They ravaged my soul like wolves, and there's no way I can ever put it back together again."

I can't help it. I have to touch him, even at the risk of him pulling back. And so I slowly reach out and press my hand gently over his. For a moment he says nothing, and I fear I've made a mistake. Then he says, "I get flashbacks. I have dreams. What I don't have anymore are relationships. She— they—twisted sex around. They made it something hard and desperate, but damned if I don't need it. The release. The tension. That edge of control. I need it. I just *need*."

"I don't understand."

He shakes his head. "Maybe I don't either. They turned sex into a battle. A fight, and if I'm not in control—I *have* to be in control— then the dark rises. The terror that I might lose myself again. And I can't go there. I can't risk it. I can't do it."

I don't understand what he means by any of this, but the pain is real. And I got a taste of that need for control in the way he pushed me against the wall, the feel of his hand against my throat, holding me still. "Have you talked to anyone?"

"Only everyone under the sun. They tell me it's normal. That it's PTSD. That I can work through it. But I've tried. Seven years I've been trying. It never gets better. It never fucking gets any better. At least after I met Marjorie—after I started sessions with her girls—at least then the nightmares stopped."

"Red..." His words are breaking my heart.

His expression is fierce. "This is who I am now. I've accepted that. But I'm not taking you down with me."

"I still don't understand. What happened to you?"

He's silent for so long I think that he's not going to tell me, then he says, "We were assigned a mission to intercept a splinter cell of a terrorist organization that was using human trafficking as a source of capital."

I nod, remembering the look on his face when Mario had mentioned that Stark Security was working on a human trafficking case, but I say nothing. Just wait for him to continue.

"It was six of us from the SOC. We were trying to track the splinter group, break them, and rescue as many victims as possible. At the same time, a small group of flight attendants had banded together to educate their peers about how to spot trafficking victims and get them safely from their captors. The group was growing, gaining interest from other airlines, and several from the group were asked to host seminars, basically spread the word."

I stay silent, but nod for him to continue.

"Intel told us the group was attracting attention from trafficking organizations that weren't happy with their results. For obvious reasons. So the SOC put an agent undercover with them. Her name was Lisa, and because of the nature of the work, we would meet up on occasion when she was between flights. She was deep cover, none of the other people at the airlines knew that she was anything other than what she appeared to be. But I did. We talked, we started dating."

I feel a ping of jealousy, and hate myself for it.

I say nothing, though, except to urge him to go on even though my stomach is twisting uncomfortably. I know this story isn't going to end well.

He tilts his head, cracking his neck, as if he can't speak until he releases that tension. "We were a year into the job when we finally identified the leaders of the cell and their base just inside the Romanian border. The job was infiltration and capture. The powers that be wanted the leaders alive so we could get more intel."

"Were you leading the team?"

He shakes his head. "No. That was Johnny. A good man. A good leader. But in the end, his skill, our team's training, the fact that we had right on our side—none of it mattered. My entire team was captured, and they killed Johnny straight away. One bullet, right between the eyes."

I wince.

"And the kicker? They simultaneously kidnapped three of the flight attendants who were on a layover, Lisa included."

"Red, I'm so sorry."

I'm not even sure he hears me. His voice is flat as he continues. "We were held hostage for I think two weeks before they started killing the rest of us off. I'm not sure. Time blurs, but for all that time, I was strapped to a chair."

Tears prick my eyes as I picture that horrible scene.

"I lived in that chair for at least a month, maybe longer. My ass was raw from the excrement I was sitting in, I was in constant pain, the world a constant haze. I think I was unconscious most of the time, floating somewhere between this world and God knows where."

He looks at me. I try not to react. And it takes all of my effort not to let the tears fall down my cheeks. But I don't want to interrupt him. I don't want to give him any reason to stop talking.

"They started killing off my companions. Some got off easy with a bullet to the head. Others were tortured. One man was flayed alive."

He draws a deep breath. "When it was just me

and the women, they took me out of the chair. They cleaned me up. They tended my wounds. They fed me. They waited until I was somewhat strong again. I thought perhaps they were going to release us with a message. That they didn't want the torture to show too dramatically." He laughs, but there's no humor in the sounds.

"I was so fucking wrong. All they were doing was making sure I was fully cognizant when they went on to the next step in their plan."

"What did they do?" The question is a whisper, and I'm certain I don't really want to hear the answer.

"They forced me to watch as they raped the three women. Alice, Jennifer, and Lisa. Over and over again, brutal and hard. They killed Alice and Jennifer. One guy was fucking Alice, and another came up and sliced her neck, but not before he left the blade pressed there so that she knew what was coming. Jennifer got it easier. A man came up from behind and blew her brains out. So at least she wasn't any more scared than she already was."

He's been looking down, but now he meets my eyes again. "They made me watch all of it. Every single one. Told me it would be worse for them if I tried to look away. I believed them."

"Every day they would tell me that they were going to kill me too. That if I didn't join them—if I didn't use my skills to help them, that's what they would do." He makes another raw noise in his throat. "They told me they knew that I never would, but that I needed to know that I had an out. A true, legitimate way to save my life. But I wasn't choosing it. I was asking for the pain, and that made it my fault not theirs."

He draws in breath and arches back, as if trying to stretch. As if the weight of these memories has pulled his body into a small, tight ball and he has to have release.

"Do you want me to keep going?"

I nod. Then I shake my head. Both answers are true. Then I say, "I want to understand. If you're willing to tell me, I'll listen to anything you say."

The tears I've tried to hold back are falling now. There's nothing I can do about that. He reaches over and gently brushes one away, and that only makes me cry all the more.

When he leans back, he rubs his palms over the scruff of his thin beard. "I don't know why they picked me to survive. Maybe they knew that I'd been dating Lisa. They knew she was undercover, though I have no idea how they learned that. But whatever the reasons, soon, it was just Lisa and me."

"Were you together at least? Could you talk to her?"

He shakes his head. "No. They only brought us

into the same room to watch each other being tortured. Mine was water."

I frown, not understanding what he means, but he continues.

"I was tied to the chair like I told you. They would strap me down so tight then they would pick me up, turn me over and dump me into a water barrel. Just leave me there."

He meets my eyes. "When I saw the video of what they did to Mel..."

He trails off with a shudder, and I feel sick. He must've almost lost his shit seeing that after what happened to him.

"Every day—every goddamn day—I wished I had a knife. I'd always carried one habitually. Still do. But they'd stripped me, so my lifelong habit was fucking useless.

"Every day, I'd tell myself that if I had one, even just a three inch blade, I could have gotten free. Killed every last one of those motherfuckers, and gotten me and Lisa out."

His throat moves as he swallows, and his eyes are glassy with tears. "I don't know if I would have managed or not, but it didn't matter. I didn't have my knife. And even if I did, I don't know that I would have been able to get to it. There was an opportunity once or twice that maybe, if I'd been careful and clever, I could have retrieved a knife hidden in my clothes. But of course, I didn't have my clothes. When they didn't leave us naked, Lisa and I were wearing rags. Literally rags tied around our bodies."

"How did you get out? Did Lisa surv—" I stop the question. I see the answer in his eyes.

"They tried to make me rape her. They couldn't do it. But oh, God, what they did. I—"

He turns his face away, and I have never seen such a look of agony in my life.

"When I refused, they gutted her. I'm not even going to—" He draws a breath. "They killed her in the most horrible way. And all I could think was that I should have been able to save her."

"No. None of this was your fault. They're the bad guys."

"If I'd only had a knife. Hell, if only I'd had a damn cyanide capsule."

I shiver. "Then you wouldn't be here now."

His smile is infinitely sad. "No, I wouldn't be. And Lisa would still be dead. And wishing things were different doesn't change anything. It was hell, and for the rest of my life I have to know that I lived through hell."

"Yes," I say. "You *lived*." I shift so that I'm sitting upright and take both his hands. "You survived, Red. It's horrible that you're the only one who did, but that's not your fault. That's their fault. You survived. And that's amazing."

I lean back again. "Will you tell me how you survived? Were you rescued?"

"I escaped." His voice is ripped. Exhausted. As if he's back in that torture chamber. "After almost a year, I finally escaped. And it wasn't even because I'm so damn special as an agent. If I was that special, I wouldn't have gotten caught in the first place."

"Do not say that," I interrupt. "It is not your fault any more than it's the fault of the rest of the members on your team. You don't blame them, do you?"

He shoots me a sideways look. "No. You're right. Of course I don't. And no, it wasn't our fault. There were a lot of things that contributed to our capture, but most were out of our control. But as for how I escaped, they got lazy."

"Lazy?"

"They were planning on killing me soon, I knew that. They were about to move locations and leave me behind in the rubble as a message. But a guard got careless. And I got lucky."

I shift on the couch, leaning forward.

"He came by himself, and when he bent to unchain me so that they could wash me again, I managed to strangle him. Somehow, I got the keys off his body. The rest was—is—a blur. I remember bits and pieces. I know I got to their weapons room, and I loaded up. At that point, I didn't care what happened to me, and I fell into a frenzy. All I cared about was killing them. What happened to me wasn't even an issue."

I hug myself, terrified for him even though I know that he got out alive.

"I got as many as I could on my way to the exit where they'd set up the detonator. And the last thing I managed to do was bring down the building and kill the rest of them."

"I'm glad you killed them." I frown, remembering something. "The other night, you talked about a woman. You kept saying *she* and *her*. What about her? Did she die, too?"

"She did, the bitch."

I think he's going to stay silent and not tell me about what she did, but after a long pause, he continues. "She was the reason they cleaned me periodically. She kept me like a pet."

I can hear the disgust in his voice.

"She chained me to her bed. She used me. I'm not going to get any more detailed than that, except to say that she got what she wanted, and I will be forever disgusted that I let her have it, that I couldn't fight my own body's reaction. She stole every bit of my control. And Jo, that's not something I'll ever let happen again." He swallows. "It's not something I can. When I try—if I try—there are flashbacks. Memories. I can't."

I hear the terror of the past in his voice and reach out for him. "I get it. It's PTSD, right?"

He nods. "So they tell me. But that doesn't really matter, does it? She made me who I am now. This isn't who I want to be."

"I don't know," I say, trying to lighten the moment. "A man who can do what you did—who escaped like that—seems to me a man like that deserves to be in control."

"Don't," he says. "Don't joke about it. I'm not talking about control with little velvet ropes you buy from some kitschy store that sells flavored lube."

"I know," I say. "I'm sorry. It was a stupid thing to say. But I also think you're too hard on yourself. You've been through hell and back. You deserve whatever you need. It doesn't make you a bad person, and it doesn't mean you're going to hurt me." I lick my lips. "That's what this boils down to, isn't it? You're afraid you're going to hurt me."

"No. Yes. But also no. I'm afraid I'm going to use you."

"Then do. That's why you see call girls, right? You use them to work through all this when it gets to be too much."

He swallows, then barely nods.

"So don't use them. Use me. Isn't it obvious, Red? I want you to."

His chuckle is completely mirthless. "It's not that simple, Jo."

"But maybe it is that simple. You don't scare me, Red. You have control in spades."

He breathes in, a long, deep breath through his nose. "I told you all this because you deserve to know. Not because there's an attraction bubbling up between us. Because honestly it's more than attraction, and I think you know that. I love you, Jo. I always have. But," he adds as he rises off the sofa, "that doesn't mean I can have you."

CHAPTER SEVENTEEN

"A laser sight? You're telling me that someone actually aimed a gun with a laser sight at your chest?" Abby stares at me, looking both appalled and in awe. "And Red jumped in front of you?" She closes her hands over her heart "Oh my God. That's like something out of an action movie. You must have been freaking terrified."

"I was," I tell her. "But don't act like it's such a big deal. You told me the story about your creepy stalker. A shiny red dot on my chest was nothing in comparison to what you went through."

Abby shakes her head. "No comparing ordeals. No one comes out the winner in that game."

We're sitting in Emma's living room on the stone hearth in front of her fireplace. It's an adorable cottage in Venice Beach which, according to Abby and Emma's sister Eliza, has tighter secu-

rity than the building inside the Tower of London
that guards the crown jewels.

All in all, it really is a great venue for Abby's
bachelorette party. It is not however, the campy,
trashy-looking strip club we'd been planning on.

"I'm really sorry that Red bullied you into
changing venues."

Abby brushes it off. "Don't be silly. He didn't
bully me. Although Renly was very happy we
decided to move it."

Renly, I know, had specifically declined to have
a stripper at his party. Abby, however, made clear
she didn't intend to be so pure. She'd talked about
tradition, then shrugged, saying that if Renly's ego
couldn't take it, well that was his problem.

"Best sex I've ever had after I told him that,"
she'd told me later. "Guess he had something to
prove."

"Still, I feel bad," I say now. "I can't say that a
strip club is my thing, but it sounded like campy
good fun."

Once again, Abby brushes away my words.
"Oh, don't you worry. There will be hot campy
goodness. Emma's seen to that."

I sweep my gaze across the room, finding
Emma talking to her sister, Eliza, along with Nikki
Stark and Jamie Hunter, Ryan's wife. I don't know
either woman well, though we've chatted a few
times when I've bumped into them at the distillery.

Nikki, of course, is the woman whose life Red saved in that horrible hostage situation two Christmases ago in New York.

I recognize a few more women as well. Abby's lifelong friend Lilah is chatting with Leah, another Stark Security agent, and a woman I don't recognize, with pale blond hair and cornflower blue eyes. I've met Lilah a few times now. She's a wisp of a woman, petite and delicate, with a biting wit that belies her sweet appearance.

"Who's Lilah talking to?"

"Oh, that's Xena. She's Liam's wife. Or maybe his girlfriend. I'm not sure, but it's obvious they're together with or without the paper."

I sigh, thinking that maybe the paper doesn't mean that much anyway. It didn't for Mel and me.

The thought makes me think of Red, just a few blocks away. The men moved their venue as well, deciding that they would rather be closer to us just in case there was a problem. Originally they were going to be at the distillery, but now they're down the street at Blacklist, a popular Venice Beach bar.

I lean forward to refresh my drink from the whiskey bottle that's sitting on the floor in front of the fireplace. "Xena used to work for Ellie Love, right?" I ask referring to the pop star who's taken all the charts by storm.

"Oh yeah. I think she may still. I'm not sure. But I know she does consulting for Stark Security."

That surprises me.

"Yeah," Abby continues when I say as much. "Renly said she's been a huge help on this trafficking operation they're chasing."

"That seems weird. What does her music background have to do with trafficking?"

"Nothing. It's all about *her* background."

I make a *whooshing* motion over my head, and Abby winces.

"Dammit, I really shouldn't talk and drink," she says. "I'm sure she doesn't mind if you know, but I still fucked up."

"You're saying she was trafficked? Or almost was?"

"Sorta. It's a horrible story," Abby says, "but I'll let her tell it to you one day. The good news is that it all worked out, and she ended up with Liam in the process."

I think about Liam, an absolutely gorgeous black man who looks like he could as easily be starring in movies as working at Stark Security. He's tall and broad, and must completely dwarf Xena, who's petite and bubbly.

"I was hoping to get the chance to meet Denny. You've become pretty close with her, right?"

"Yeah, I'm sorry she didn't make it. Apparently her little one's come down with a cold. She's only working part-time these days. Since she's a new mom, she wants to spend as much time as possible

with her little girl before she's school-age. And
Mason, her husband, only works a few select jobs.
He says he wants as much of home and hearth and
sex—his words—that he can get. But I figured he's
earned the right to back off if anyone has."

I take a sip of my whiskey, then wave to Emma
who's pointing at a whiteboard she's just pulled
out. *Dirty Pictionary* is written across the top in
neat block handwriting. I flash her a thumbs up and
then signal that we'll just be a minute.

"It looks like it's about time for the games, so
tell me quick what's going on with Mason that he
earned the right."

Abby pushes to her feet "You should ask him.
Or Denny. Suffice it to say that whatever drama
you have with Red, it must be a cakewalk compared
to what they went through."

She claps her hand over her mouth "Oh, God, I
went and put my foot in it again."

I don't have a clue what she's talking about.

She winces. "I shouldn't be talking about you
two like that."

I laugh. "In case you missed the memo, I'm the
one who dragged you aside at your own party, and
told you." I'd laid it all out for her, really needing a
female friend to dump on. It was only after I'd
dragged her into my emotional mess that I told her
about the laser sight and other terrifying things.

I know. But—"

"What?"

"I'm just happy for you and Red, but I know it must be weird. Feeling that way about him with what happened to Mel." She shrugs. "I've been drinking too much, and I'm sorry if I'm bringing up weird memories or making you feel awkward."

"You're not. Really." The truth is, my feelings for Red seem more right to me than anything has in a long time. So it's not awkwardness I feel, it's frustration for the way he's pushing me away, and anger at the people who messed him up so much that he doesn't trust himself to be with me.

I don't say that, though. Today needs to be about Abby and Renly, and I take her hand and tug her toward the Pictionary area. Emma comes over with scorecards in her hands. "You two okay?"

"We're fine," I assure her. "We somehow got on the topic of my husband. A sad topic, and not suitable for a wedding shower," I say with a stern look towards Abby.

"Nonsense," Emma says. "It's all the cycle right? And I didn't know him, but I doubt he wanted you to sit home. He'd want you to remember the good times. To honor him and enjoy your life. Let this be a reminder of how short it can be. Believe me, I've danced with death more times than I can count. Don't sit it out when life invites you onto the floor."

I'm smiling when she finishes that speech and I

reach forward and pull her into a hug, not even asking if it was okay. Thankfully, she hugs me back. From what I've heard about Emma, you can't be too sure about that kind of thing.

"And on that wise counsel," she says, "it's now time to turn to something more base."

"Pictionary?"

"That's next," Emma says, taking Abby's hand. "First, we need to put you in the Princess seat."

"Oh my God," I say. "It's stripper time?"

Abby gives me a look filled with both anticipation and trepidation as Emma leads her away to a chair that's been decorated as a throne.

Then someone starts the music, and a dude dressed like a fireman struts into the room. Assuming fire stations let half-naked men work there.

It's so campy and stupid that I can't help but laugh, especially when he starts to do his bump-and-grind routine right in front of Abby's face.

The man's built, I'll give him that. But the more he starts to tease and play—the more clothing he starts to peel away—the more I find myself thinking of Red, and hoping that somehow we can make this thing between us work out.

CHAPTER EIGHTEEN

"—Friends for years."

Red blinked, realizing he'd zoned out. "Sorry, what?"

He and Renly were standing by the bar at Blacklist, waiting for the harried bartender to come take their order for the few drinks and snacks they needed to refresh their table.

"I said it looks like we're both going to end up with our best friends," Renly said.

Red shot his brother a sideways look. "You're the one who lucked out, buddy. I'm not going to end up with Jo. No way would I saddle her with the likes of me."

Renly took a sip of his beer as he studied Red, the inspection taking so long that Red started to squirm. "You ever going to tell me what happened?"

Red stirred the cherry in his Coke. "Probably not."

"Fair enough." He grabbed a handful of nuts, then chewed them slowly. Finally, he said, "Can I offer you some free advice?"

"This is your bachelor party, bro. Not a therapy session for me." He glanced at the table, hoping one of the other men would come to his rescue, but they were all laughing and chowing down on the cheese fries and nachos they'd ordered.

"You want the damn advice or not?"

Red sighed. "Lay it on me."

"Don't do what Mom did. Don't wait decades to make the right decision."

Red shook his head. "It's not the same."

Renly scooped one of the cheese fries off of his plate and popped it in his mouth. "Not directly, no." He chewed and swallowed. "But ask yourself this—what are you scared of? Deep down, do you really believe that Jo can't deal with your shit? Or are you afraid that *you* won't be able to deal with it if you let yourself take the risk and she says no?"

"Renl—"

His brother held up a hand. "All I'm saying is that I don't know what's going on with you, not completely. But I have an idea. We know each other well enough. And let me tell you, if it's the latter, then you're a fool. Because Jo's a hell of a lot stronger than you think."

Red tried again to get a word in, but Renly didn't give him the chance. "And if she does cut and run? Well, at least you have your answer."

"And I'll have lost my best friend."

Renly smiled, and Red kicked himself for what he'd just revealed. Because his brother had nailed it. The fear wasn't so much that Jo would bolt, although that possibility did terrify him. The fear was that if she did, then the most solid and best thing in his universe would be ripped from him.

But Renly was right about something else, too. Because by holding back, Red was cheating both himself and Jo out of the chance of finding out.

God, he hated it when his twin was right.

"You know you're a pain in my ass?"

Renly grinned. "You're welcome."

Not that drilling down on his particular neuroses solved his ability to pay attention that night. Despite the fact that they were supposed to be feting his brother before he got married, Red kept having the same damn problem. He couldn't keep his mind on the conversation.

With effort, he forced himself to tune back in just as Mario was saying, "—ridiculously cool, right? And Renly, my man, I owe you big time."

"The hell you do," Simon said. "You should run far and fast."

"What did I miss?" Red asked. Renly shot him a knowing look, but answered anyway.

"Mario's singing my praises because I'm sending him to Francesca's house on Monday to check out her security system. I was going to handle it, but, hey, honeymoon."

Across the table, Mario beamed. "Seriously, Renly. You are the coolest."

"Just promise me you won't drool on her. Very uncool."

The rest of the table laughed, but Simon only shook his head.

Red considered asking the new guy what his problem with Hollywood was, but decided he had problems enough of his own. Instead, he kicked back and sipped his Coke, half-listening to the others laugh and tell jokes. They teased Renly and praised Abby, and the conversation ebbed and flowed. But Red couldn't manage to keep his bearings. Instead, his mind drifted, and he found himself looking out over the street, watching the tourists and residents stroll by.

The restaurant boasted doors that folded back, allowing the place to essentially be an open-air restaurant. He imagined himself and Jo strolling along the sidewalk, remembering that they'd done just that in college, coming down here to go walking on the beach or roller skating on the paved path.

He should bring her back here. They could—

He saw her. A flash of dark hair. That slightly

crooked smile that on some women would look cute, but on her just seemed evil. *The woman.*

No.

He blinked. Because it couldn't be her. He closed his eyes, then looked over again, and sure enough, she was gone.

Fuck.

His damn mind was playing tricks, and it was his own fault. He should never have told Jo about the woman. Talking about her had brought her back into his mind. Had given her life again, even though he knew damn good and well that she was dead. He'd seen the explosion, the rubble. There was no way she survived.

She lived now only in his head, but apparently that was enough to drive him crazy.

He lifted his glass to take a sip of Coke, then realized he was shaking. He tried to stop, but couldn't seem to manage it. He had to go look; he had to be sure.

He bent over and tapped his brother's shoulder. "I'll be right back." Then, before Renly even had a chance to respond, he stepped out of the restaurant and moved to the middle of the street, ignoring the cars that honked, and the people that shouted for him to get the fuck out of the road.

But he saw no one. Not a single person who looked like her. It had been his imagination. It must have been.

He headed back in, telling himself to chill the fuck out. And for a little bit, he was actually able to take his own damn advice. Half an hour later, he'd relaxed, and was kicked back, grinning as Quincy shared how he and Eliza found each other again, that British accent of his making the undercover-at-a-sex-party mission sound pretty damn classy.

That's when he saw her again.

Shit.

He turned away, then back again. Nothing. Once again, she was gone.

He was seeing ghosts. He was surrounded by goddamn ghosts. He had to be.

The woman was dead. She and the men who'd helped her.

But what if she wasn't a ghost?

He told himself that he was being paranoid, but he couldn't take the risk. He bent toward Renly. "I have to go."

"You okay?"

"I'm antsy about being away from Jo under the circumstances. It's probably my imagination, but I'm not going to second guess myself."

Renly looked around the table. "Want us to come with you?"

He shook his head. "No. I'm sure it's nothing. Just my own paranoia. But I'm not taking chances with her."

"Fair enough."

He clapped his brother on the shoulder. "Next time I see you, you'll be a married man."

"I know. Isn't it fabulous?"

Red had to agree. Because he didn't think he'd ever seen a man look happier than Renly did in that moment.

He thought of Jo as he headed out, then walked down the street toward Emma's house, his brother's face filling his thoughts. That's when Red knew how happy he'd look if only Jo could be his.

Seeing Renly was like looking in mirror, after all.

What he still didn't know was if he could ever have her. If he would ever be able to truly open up. And even if he did, he didn't know if she could handle his shit.

His brother was right. Red was too scared to push.

But he'd learned one thing for certain tonight, if he didn't, he'd never know what could have been. And damned if he couldn't live with that either.

CHAPTER NINETEEN

B ecause my friends have absolutely no class, we're playing pin the cock on the porn star when I look over and see Red step in through Emma's front door. His brows are furrowed, and I don't think it's because of the ridiculousness of the game.

I hurry to him, stumbling a little because I've had too much to drink. "Is something wrong?"

"We need to go."

My stomach twists. "What happened?"

"Nothing. It's fine."

"Then why do we have to go?"

"Dammit, Jo, please. Let's go."

I study his face, see the genuine concern there, and nod. "Just give me a second to say goodbye."

I make the circle, say goodbye to my friends old

and new, then give Abby an extra tight hug. "I'll think about you tomorrow at one," I tell her. That's when their ceremony before the judge is scheduled for. "You'll be a married woman when I see you again."

Her grin is wide and her face sparkles with happiness. "I know. Isn't it awesome?"

"It really is," I agree, then hurry back to Red.

He seems less agitated now. "I'm sorry about pulling you away," he says as we step outside and start walking to his car. "But I have a bad feeling."

"Why? You said nothing happened." I glance around, looking at every stranger. When he doesn't answer, I shift my attention back to him. "Red? Tell me what's going on."

He looks sideways at me, but doesn't stop walking. "I thought I saw her."

"Her?" I stop on the sidewalk. "The woman in Romania?"

He's a few steps ahead now, and has to backtrack to me. We get few looks from beach-clad twenty-somethings who have to step around us, but I don't care.

"The woman you killed?" I whisper. "That's not possible."

"Of course it's not possible," he snaps. "But I fucking saw her."

"I believe you. I'm sorry." I take his hand. "But

you're not in that room anymore. All of that is over."

He draws in a breath, then nods. I step closer and give him a hug. I'm tentative, not sure he wants to be touched, but he goes all in, pulling me hard against me, as if he never wants to let me go.

"Maybe it was my imagination. Maybe it really was a goddamn ghost. I don't know. But it spooked me." He pushes back, his eyes searching my face. "Do you know why?"

"No."

He draws in a breath, and I notice him glance around, checking our surroundings. It's the third time I've noticed it on this short walk, but instead of being nervous, his alertness makes me feel safe.

"Red?" I press.

"Because of you," he says. "It spooked me because of you."

I gape at him, completely confused. "I'm sorry. I don't know what—"

"No," he says, twining his fingers with mine. "It's a good thing. Don't you get it? I died in that room."

I have no idea what he's talking about, and he's starting to really scare me. I tug him to the side, next to a small shop window. "What are you talking about?"

His shoulders rise and fall as he takes one deep

breath, then another. "I'm trying to say that I've been dead for years. I'm trying to tell you that you were the one who brought me back to life."

I can only stare at him. "Oh," I finally say, the word too small for the emotions rising in me. I feel a little bit like the Grinch, my heart expanding inside my chest. "Well, that's good, isn't it?"

His smile flickers. "It is. But it's hard. It's fucking hard walking and feeling and loving. And risking," he adds, his gaze meeting mine before flicking away.

"What are you risking?"

"You."

I shake my head, once again not understanding what he means.

"I'm terrified that you can't handle the man I am. The man they made me into. But, Jo—I swear to you, I will do everything I can to be the man you need."

"Are you saying you'd try to be something else for me?"

"I'll be whatever you need, if only I can."

A knife-edge of anger shoots through me, and before I even know what I'm doing, I've reached out and slapped his face.

He staggers back a step, his expression an odd combination of anger and bewilderment. "What the hell was that for?"

I take a step toward him, my own anger still hot. "I don't want that. God, Red, you are so dense."

Maybe it's the alcohol that's fueling my fury, but I give him a hard shove with the heel of my hand. A passing couple gives us a wide berth, and the whole situation is so ridiculous, I almost laugh.

"I want you, you idiot. You're messed up? I get that. But guess what, so is everyone. Maybe not as much as you, I'll give you that. But I need you, Red. I want you. I want you to be whoever you are. And," I add with fierce determination, "I want you to take whatever you need."

"I believe you," he says. "But you don't know—"

"No. Just no. God, you've pissed me off."

I start walking again, and he falls in beside me. We're silent until we reach the car. As I open the passenger door, I look at him over the hood. "Don't you have any faith in me at all?"

Confusion flickers across his face. "Jo, I—"

"Just get in," I tell him, then slide in myself. Then I sit in the passenger seat with my arms crossed over my chest.

For a full five minutes, he says nothing. We just sit in the car. When he does speak, he doesn't look at me. "I'm scared, Jo. I'm scared you don't want to give what I need, and I'm scared I can't ask you for it anyway."

I'm not sure if it's relief or anticipation that

bubbles through me. Probably both. "Well, we're just going to have to work through that, aren't we?" I nod at the steering wheel. "But we're not going to figure it out here. Let's go."

I flash him what I hope is a seductive smile. "I have an idea."

To his credit, he doesn't argue. And fortunately, traffic is light, because I'm ready to be home. I want his mouth on mine. I want his body against me. I want to feel him inside me. I want to lose myself in his arms and forget all the horror that's been happening around us. Mostly, though, I just want him.

And I think I know the way to get him.

As soon as we're inside, I shut the door behind us, then grab his hand and yank him toward me. I rise up on my toes, get right in his face, and say, "Pay me."

If I wasn't so determined, his expression would make me laugh. He takes a step backwards, tugging his hand free. "What the hell are you talking about?"

"That's what you do, right? That's why you have Marjorie brokering girls for you. And I bet you don't have any trouble asking—no, *telling*—them what you want." I flash a winsome smile. "So pay me, and I'll do what ever you say because I have to. The customer is always right, isn't he?"

He starts to shakes his head, but I don't let him

get away with that. "I'm serious. And honestly, I can use the money. These floors need to be refinished, and there's a leak in the attic. So you can help fund my house repair kitty."

"Jo—"

"How much do you usually pay those girls?"

The corner of his mouth quirks, but he answers. "More than I should."

"Yeah, yeah. But how much? Five-hundred?"

There's no humor in his laughter. "Jo, give it a rest."

"A grand?"

"Dammit—"

"Fine. You can do whatever you want to me," I say, trailing my fingertip down his chest and then grabbing his waistband. I give it a yank, forcing him to stumble toward me. "But it'll cost you five grand."

He moves like lightening, caging me against the wall, his face close to mine, his hands on either side of me, his body so close I can feel his heat. "Dammit, Jo, stop it. You have no idea what you're offering."

Anger lashes through me. "The hell I don't. I'm offering *me,* you idiot. What do I have to do to prove it? This?"

I reach for his fly, then suck in air when I feel how hard he is under the khaki of his slacks. I glance up, meeting his eyes defiantly, then nimbly undo the button. I work the zipper down, then slide my fingers in to stroke his cock.

Or I try to, anyway.

In one swift motion, he pulls me away toward him, then spins me around so that my arms are pinned above my head and my cheek is pressed to the wall.

"Is this what you want?" he asks as one hand pins my arms above my head and the other yanks down my skirt. It's a floral print peasant skirt with an elastic band, and I gasp as he shoves it down so that it pools around my feet, leaving me only in a pair of pale blue panties and my blouse.

"This?" he continues, roughly spreading my legs before thrusting one hand down the back of my panties. His thumb presses against my ass as his fingers find my core. I gasp as he thrusts deep inside me, then leans in, his mouth against my ear. "Should I fuck your ass, baby? My cock and fingers inside you at the same time, fucking you so hard your tits are bruised from the wall, your cheek scraped because you can't fucking escape from me?"

My pussy clenches around him, and I'm so turned on I think I'll melt. "Yes. Oh, God, Red, yes. Please."

"Jo," he says, more of a groan than a word, and I

sigh with pleasure, only to gasp again when he spins me around to face him, his hands caging me on either side of my shoulders. I'm breathing hard, and so is he. "You don't know what you're getting into with me."

"I do," I say. "I'm getting *you*. All of you. Do you think I want some fake version of the man I love? Quit worrying about me, Red, and just be who you are, dammit. You cross a line, and I swear I will tell you. But," I add, "I don't think you will."

His breath tickles my face, but he doesn't move. I reach for one of his hands, then press his palm over my breast. Then I slide it down until his fingers reach the band of my panties. I lead him under teasing my clit with his fingers. "Please, Red," I whisper, closing my eyes as his fingers move on their own, sliding over my folds. "Yes, more. I'm begging you."

I hear his low, harsh groan, then whimper myself when he pulls his hand away. I'm about to protest—I'm so damn frustrated—when I feel the pressure of his hands on my breasts over my blouse. I open my eyes as his fingers grip the edges where the buttons are fastened. One quick tug, and he's ripped it open, and I hear buttons pinging on the floor.

I gasp, then moan as he yanks down one cup of my bra, exposing my breast. His fingers tease my already sensitive nipple, and I bite my lip, forcing myself not to beg as more pleasure seeps through me, pooling between my legs.

As if he's reading my mind, his other hand slides down, his fingers going deep inside me. "Christ, you feel good," he murmurs, then closes his mouth over mine in a deep, brutal kiss, so hot and demanding I'm utterly destroyed.

When he pulls back, I'm gasping for breath, unable to gather myself because of the way his fingertips continue to tease my nipple even as his fingers play with my pussy.

I'm desperately wet, and my body clenches around him, wanting all of him. Wanting every-thing. "Don't stop," I say, writhing against his hand, then crying out when he twists my nipple hard, the sensation of pain mixed with pleasure sending sparks racing through my body, sensitizing every inch of me and making my pussy clench around his fingers.

"Did that hurt?"

"Yes," I whisper.

"Did you like it?"

"God, yes." My eyes are closed, but I open them now. He's looking at me with such lust and passion, my legs go weak.

Then the corner of his mouth curves up. "With me," he says, then leads me to my bedroom.

"Do you have any toys?" he asks, then chuckles.

"What's funny?"

"*Now* you blush?"

"Mel didn't like to play like that," I admit, realizing that my cheeks really are burning.

"*Mel* didn't?"

I shake my head, holding his gaze. "I wanted to try things. All kinds of things," I add lifting my chin. "You haven't even come close to the things I thought about."

"I'll keep that in mind. Show me what you have."

It takes me a second to realize he means the toys, but when I do, I head to the bookshelf and pull down an oversized copy of *Anna Karenina*

His brows rise.

"It's a fake," I say, lifting the cover to reveal a combination lock. I dial in the code, then open it to reveal a compartment with a vibrator, a blindfold, and some silk cord. I shrug. "I told you. Pretty lame."

"It's a start," he says. "Take off the rest of your clothes, then get on the bed. On your knees. Your ass toward me."

I do, my nipples tightening simply from the command in his voice.

He tells me to scoot closer to the headboard, and when I comply, he comes behind me, then blindfolds me. "No fair," I protest. "I'm completely naked and you're still dressed. I didn't get to see a thing."

"Arguing?" he asks.

"No, sir," I answer, and hear his responding chuckle.

He tells me to bend forward so that my chest is on the bed with my arms in front, but my ass still in the air. I do, and he uses the silk cord to bind my wrists to the headboard.

"I like that," he murmurs, trailing a finger from my clit all the way to my ass. I bite my lower lip, wondering if he's going to fuck me there, and surprised by how much I want him too.

"I'm going to spank you, baby. And then I'm going to fuck you."

"Yes, please," I murmur, then bite my lip when he bends over me, his cock pressed hard against my rear as he reaches for one breast. With his other hand, he fingers my pussy. I moan as he twists my nipple, then sigh with pleasure as he teases my clit. "You're so wet, baby. Let's see if we can't take you to the edge."

I feel the bed shift, then the stroke of his palm against my rear. I bite my lip, certain what's coming, but unprepared for the sweet sting when it finally arrives. I've never been spanked before, but I can't deny the way my body reacts to the sting, my nipples tightening, my pussy throbbing, and then a warm tingling sensation coursing through me as he rubs the sore spot with the palm of his hand.

"You like that," he says, his tone suggesting he wasn't sure.

"Yes," I say simply. "Are you going to do it again?"

"Do you want me to?"

"Yes, please."

He doesn't answer, but I hear his sharp intake of breath. He spanks me again, that sting followed by the sweet pleasure of his soothing ministrations. Again, then again, a bit harder each time until my body is on fire and my pussy is so wet and needy I'm fighting not to beg.

As if he can read my mind, he moves behind me, then thrusts his cock into me, so hard and fast that I gasp from the combination of pain and pleasure. He bends over, one hand cupping my sensitive breast and his other beneath me teasing my clit as he fucks me so hard I'll probably have friction burns on my knees. And I want that—oh, how I want it. This sensual assault, the pain and the pleasure, and the visible marks to show that, finally, he surrendered and claimed me.

"That's it, baby," he says. He's close, I'm certain, and so am I. My body poised to explode, to shatter all around him. "Come for me," he murmurs, and it's as if my body has no choice but to bend to his will, because that's when I explode, the world shattering around me as I lose myself to the power of the pleasure from this mind-blowing orgasm.

Finally, I collapse, Red on top of me. I'm breathing deep, lost in a haze, and I only barely notice when he removes my blindfold and unties my wrists. I feel his body shift and realize he's stretched out beside me, but I don't move or open my eyes. Not yet.

All I want to do is stay here, boneless and sated. But at the same time, I want more.

I want it all.

I roll over, then push myself up and move to straddle him. His eyes flicker open, and he smiles at me. "Well, hello there."

"You held back," I accuse.

Something flickers in his eyes. "Maybe. A little."

I slide down so that I can feel his cock against my ass. I grind against him, my hands flat on his chest. "I want more."

His grin is slow and utterly kissable. He cups my ass and squeezes. "I can go another round."

He starts to roll us over, but I interrupt. "No. That's not what I meant. I want *more*."

"Jo—"

"No. No way. I've got the floor." A muscle in his cheek contracts, and I know he understands where I'm going with this. I rush to continue. "I'm not naïve. I read books. I watch movies. I live in this world. I know what it is you're into, or at least I think I do. You need to talk to me, Red. You need to tell me what you want. Because that was one hell of an amazing orgasm you gave me, but even with the ropes and the spanking, it was pretty damn vanilla."

"You don't—"

"No, I don't. Because you haven't showed me. And maybe I don't *know*, but I know enough to know you're not just into kink. We're talking hard core, right? Domination. Submission. And maybe I am naive, but I trust you, dammit. And the thing is, I have needs, too."

"Do you?" The question has an edge to it, as if he's almost afraid of what I'll say.

"You, Red. I need you. And that means that wherever you need to go, I'll follow. Not because you're forcing me to do something I don't want to do. But because I want to follow you there."

"Did you and Mel ...?"

"No." I feel my cheeks heat, which is a ridiculous reaction considering we're naked and talking about kink. "I told you. I, um, suggested stuff a couple of times, not hardcore. But..."

I trail off with a shrug.

"What?"

"It wasn't what he wanted. And ..." I hesitate, hating the fact that I need to voice this sad truth. "And even though I did want it—that edge that trust—I didn't want it with Mel. Not anymore. Maybe I never did."

I don't realize I'm crying until he reaches up and brushes away a tear.

I slide one hand up his chest over that magnificent tattoo, then press my palm over his heart. "But the thing is, Red, I'm absolutely positive that I want that with you."

CHAPTER TWENTY

I want it with you.

Her words filled him, giving him hope, but also dredging up fear.

"Why?" He had to know what she was thinking. Had to understand where she was coming from.

"Because it excites me. I want to get into your head. I want to be close to you. Don't you get it Red? I love you."

He said nothing, all he could do was look at her. All he could do was want her and wish that he was a big enough man to be able to trust that if he did what she was asking—if he took what he wanted—then she would still be there in the morning. Because she was the thing he wanted most of all.

"You're scared," she said, reading his mind as always. "You think I don't mean it."

He lifted his shoulder and let it fall. "Maybe a little."

She rolled her eyes. "Then start slow."

She rolled over, then straddled him. She put her hands on his shoulders, then drew them down to the buttons of his shirt and started to unbutton them one by one while he held his breath and wondered if his heart would ever remember to start beating again.

"We have a lifetime for you to show me just how rough you like it," she said. "Because I'm not going anywhere. I didn't fight for you seven years ago when you pushed me away, and we both missed out. I'm not missing out this time."

"Jo."

She pressed a finger to his lips. "Don't you get it? This is what I want. To know I belong to you, that you need me."

She climbed off of him, then sat up beside him, naked and completely unselfconscious. He was still mostly clothed, though his shirt was open and his cock was free from where he'd opened his fly to fuck her. He was still hard, and her words were doing a number on him. On his head and on his cock.

She reached for his hand. "I've been alone my whole life except for with you and Mel. And honestly, even though I loved Mel, it was never like this. Don't you get it? We fit. We're like a lock and a key. And you know it too," she said. "Don't you?"

He swallowed, but since he owed her the truth, he nodded.

"So don't push me away, Red. Do the opposite. Pull me closer than you ever thought you could."

He just watched her, trying to decide, knowing that the decision had already been made. He craved her too much. "I want to," he admitted. "But losing you terrifies me."

"You won't," she said softly. "But I get that you won't believe me just because I say so. So we'll do whatever you need. If that's to go slow, then I'm okay with that. You want to be vanilla for years, I'm okay with that, too."

His lips twitched.

"What?"

"Vanilla."

"That's what it's called, right?"

"It is."

"See?" she said, moving to straddle him again. "I'm already well-versed."

He started to laugh, but she put a finger over his mouth. "Maybe we try one new thing a week. Or a month. Or a year if that makes you more sure. But if you're afraid I'll leave, that I can't handle it, then you're wrong. I will give you whatever you need."

Again, he started to speak, and once again she silenced him.

"Push me to the edge, Red. I want you to. I want passion. I want tenderness. I want all of that. But I want more, too. You want me to be your sex slave? I will. You want me to be totally submissive? Fine."

She ran her hands down his chest, and his body hardened in response. He wanted to believe her. God, how he wanted to believe her.

"You don't understand what you're asking." She couldn't. Because whatever she was thinking, he undoubtedly needed it a thousand times more intense.

"That's only because you haven't shown me. But I promise, I will let you take whatever you need. I want you to, and not just because I love you … it turns me on, too," she said, and God, how he wanted to believe that.

"Jo—"

"I swear I'll tell you if it's too much. And I'm not even talking about tonight, Red. We have the rest of our lives. All I want is to be the one for you. If you need something, you crave something, you come to me." She drew a breath. "But if you really can't, then maybe we'll call Marjorie together."

His brows rose, and he wasn't quite sure he was hearing her right.

"I'm not saying it's my first choice. I'm saying

that I love you, and that I'll be whatever you need me to be. And if you need me to stand aside or be the second girl, well, we can work it out."

"That will never happen," he said. "The call, I mean—but god I love you for suggesting it."

"Does that mean you trust me? That you'll come to me? That you won't hold back?"

"Starting slow?" he said.

"Slow, fast, whatever convinces you that I can be there for you."

He nodded, not sure how in the hell he'd gotten so lucky to have her as a friend and his lover. She filled his heart. "It'll be slow," he said. "I do trust you, Jo. And God knows I need you. But we'll go slow. And only with you."

"You're sure?"

"I'm nervous," he admitted, the words coming easy because the admission was to Jo. "But I love you, baby. More, I need you. So, yeah. I'm sure. Now come here."

Her brows rose, but she complied.

"Lay across the bed, face down."

She did as he asked as he got up, then went to rummage in her bedside table drawer.

"What are you looking for?"

"Found it," he said, holding up a black Sharpie. He crossed back to her, then used it to write on her ass while she squealed with laughter.

"What are you doing?"

"An IOU," he said, capping the Sharpie. "For five grand. For services rendered tonight. From now on, though, no payment. Because I own you, baby. Don't I?"

"Yeah," she said, laughter in her eyes as she rolled over, then reached out a hand to pull him toward her. "You really do."

CHAPTER TWENTY-ONE

When I wake to sunlight streaming through the gaps in the curtains, Red is spooned against me. I sigh, lost in a pleasant haze. "I could get used to this," I murmur.

He nuzzles my hair. "Do you have any idea what a revelation you are?"

I roll over so that I'm facing him. "Thank you," I say, then continue when his brow rises. "For agreeing."

His lips twitch. "I should be thanking you for pushing."

"I pushed because I meant it," I tell him. "Promise me you haven't changed your mind. That you won't sacrifice anything you need because you think I can't handle it. I'm a big girl. I promise to say no if I need you to stop or slow down."

"I promise."

"Good. Honestly, I shouldn't even have had to say this. You should already have known. Haven't we always been there for each other?"

He chuckles. "I think you running out to get me emergency Milky Ways when I was drowning in chem final reviews is a far cry from what I want from you in bed."

I laugh. "Yeah, but you forget the most important thing." I wait until his brows raise in question. "I like both Milky Ways and sex."

He laughs, then pulls me close for a kiss, this one sweet enough not to get me riled up again.

I sigh and settle back, still facing him, which gives me a view over his shoulders to my bookcase beyond. I see the space left by *Anna Karenina*, and I sit up, looking for the booksafe that got kicked to the floor. I find it tumbled open, my vibrator still inside.

"We should go shopping," I tell him. "Let you do the selecting so that you can really take me down the rabbit hole. We could make a day of it, even get a hotel and—"

Oh, God. It couldn't be that simple. Could it?

I scramble of the bed, then go to the book, yanking it toward me. I already know the answer, but I run my finger over the lock, anyway.

"Jo? What the hell? Are you okay?" He's moving as he speaks, and now he's kneeling naked in front of me, his hand on my shoulder. I barely notice. "Jo, dammit, what's going on."

"The thing," I say. "The MacGuffin. Red, I think I know where it is."

He looks at me like I'm crazy. But I'm not crazy. I stand up, then scramble into a pair of jeans. "We have to go."

"Dammit, Jo. Talk to me. What did you realize? Where are we going?"

"The distillery," I say, tossing on a black tee without bothering about a bra. "It's the book. It's in the book."

To his credit, he doesn't slow down getting dressed, but he does shoot me a look that suggests he's concerned about my sanity.

I sigh. "About two years ago, Mel and I went to the Rose Bowl Flea Market. There was this booth that had all sorts of things that were book related. I bought that book at a booth. We each got one. I got *Anna Karenina*, and he got an old dictionary. He keeps it in his office at the distillery."

I see the moment understanding hits him.

"This has to be it, right?" I ask.

"I don't know," he says. "But right now, it's the only lead we have."

I shove my feet into a pair of canvas flats, then hurry toward the door. "Come on, let's go."

"Coming." He grabs his keys and wallet off my dresser and I hurry ahead, then disarm the security system at the panel by the front door. He reaches my side, and I pull the door open, then step out onto the porch, only to release a sharp, short scream when I see the figure standing on my front porch steps.

"Put down your weapon, Mr. Cooper."

I barely register the voice as I turn to see Red standing behind me, a handgun aimed right at Detective Amaro.

Immediately I sag with relief as the reality that it's the detective—and not the killer—standing on my stoop.

"Sorry," Red says, putting the gun on the welcome mat, then standing. "Under the circumstances you can't really blame me."

"Circumstances?" she says.

I almost wince; as far as I know, the cops believe Mel committed suicide. But Red covers the mistakes seamlessly. "Jo had a break-in. We just had the security system redone. She's a little jumpy. Add to that Mel's suicide, and I'm helping keep her safe."

"I'm sorry about the break-in," the detective says, stepping onto the porch and into the light. "Did you report it?"

I shake my head. "No. With everything that's been going on, I just wanted to put it behind me." True words. Just not a true context. I frown as I look at the detective. "Why are you here?"

"We just received some interesting information. I'd like you to come down to the station with me."

"And why is that?" Red says, before I can reply.

"Ms. Swift? I'd appreciate your cooperation?"

I glance to Red who shakes his head. "We were on our way out, obviously," I say. "What's this about?"

"Your financial situation."

I shake my head, completely baffled. "My financial situation?"

"With your husband dead, you are now a two-thirds shareholder in the distillery along with Mr. Cooper." She shifts her gaze to Red. "Nice of you to stay here, keeping the widow safe and comfortable."

"We've been friends since college, detective," he says. "I believe I told you that. All three of us. So are you going to tell us what this is regarding, or are we going to play games?"

"What did you mean by my finances?" I ask again.

"In addition to your ownership interest in the distillery, there's also the matter of the life insurance."

"Life insurance?" I repeat. "We barely have any. Just term life on each of us that we got when we got married, and not even enough to pay off this mortgage." I realize that I haven't even thought about insurance. I guess I'm supposed to file a claim or something.

I swallow back tears as I continue. "I have the policies," I tell her. "Do you need to see them?"

"That won't be necessary. I'm talking about the two million dollar policy on your husband's life that you took out three weeks ago."

"What the hell?" I take a step back, suddenly cold. "I don't know what you're talking about."

"Then it's a good thing we're going to the station isn't it? I'm sure we can get it all straightened out there."

I look over at Red, confused and scared. How the hell is there a two million dollar policy on Mel?

He takes a step forward. "Detective, are you arresting Ms. Swift?"

"As I thought I made clear, we merely want to have a conversation. Work through some questions. A quick sit-down to clear things up. It will be better for everyone in the long run."

"I'm not so sure about that," Red says. "So here's the deal. Arrest her if you want, but if you're not going to do that, then I think you need to make an appointment to see Ms. Swift with her attorney."

For a second I think that Detective Amarro is going to arrest me, just because she's annoyed with Red. But she doesn't, of course. My firm may not do criminal law, but I know enough to know that without something concrete, it would be foolish to arrest.

And there can't be anything concrete. Can there?

After a tense moment, she says that she'll be in touch, then turns and heads back to her car.

Red and I stand on the porch until she disappears down the street. Then I glance at him, my knees going weak as I sag down onto the top porch step. "I don't know anything about that much life insurance."

"I know."

"This is them, isn't it? Whoever killed Mel is playing with us."

"I think they must be."

"Who? Who's doing this? Why did they kill Mel? Why are they trying to point the police in my direction? How is that supposed to help us getting this thing back for them? It doesn't make any sense." The questions spill out as tears—from stress and fear and too damn much adrenalin—stream down my cheeks.

"Nothing makes sense," he says, taking my hand.

And in that moment, despite my wildly roiling emotions, I have to disagree with him.

Because as I looked down at our intertwined fingers, I realize that right now, in this moment, there is one thing that makes perfect sense. *Us.*

CHAPTER TWENTY-TWO

"It feels like an eternity since I've been here," Red said, unlocking the door to the tasting room. He'd already sent a text to Jessn and Charlie G, letting them know he'd be on property, but that he'd prefer not to talk today. With the beefed up security system, they'd be notified the moment he started to punch in the code. With the message, hopefully they'd abide by his wishes and not come join them.

He held the door open for Jo, then followed her in. "The police are right, you know. We three were equal before, but now this place is more yours than mine."

She slid into his arms. "Does that bother you?"

"Not as long as you're mine, too."

Her smile bloomed. "You know I am."

He looked around the business that he and Mel

had spent so many hours planning and growing. Those long years before they even had a whiskey ready for market. The hours sanding and polishing the bar to get it exactly the way they wanted. The floors they'd debated for a week. Everything down to the logo. It had been an adventure. And dammit, he missed his friend.

"I wonder if he's haunting this place." He said the question more to himself than Jo, but she answered anyway.

"If he is, it's because he wants us to avenge him. Not because he's angry with us. I'm certain of that."

They'd been traversing the tasting room, but now he paused. He hooked a finger under her chin, then tilted her head back. "I don't begrudge Mel his time with you, and I would give anything to have him back. But I agree. I think that wherever he is, he's happy for us."

"He is," she assured him, then leaned in to kiss him. "And he'll be happier when we avenge him." She glanced around, her voice rising as she said, "You hear that, Mel? I don't know what you got yourself into, but if you want to help us take these fuckers down, then give us a sign or something. They killed you and they're setting me up and if there's anything you can tell us, then now's the time."

She fell silent, and they both listened, as if their friend really was able to help them. But the room stayed silent. No small rumbles of the bottles behind the bar. No mysterious messages appearing on the glass.

Jo shot him a sideways glance. "Guess that means we're already on the right track." She took his hand. "Come on."

"The set-up won't stick," he said as they continued toward Mel's office. "You know that, right? They did it to push you harder to find this thing, but ultimately, the life insurance bullshit will fall apart." They hadn't talked about it on the drive because she hadn't wanted to. But he knew she was freaked out that someone had gone so far as to try to make her look dirty.

"I know. Or, at least, I think I know." They paused outside Mel's office. "I'm not worried about that. Not much anyway." Her lips pursed, and he could tell she was fighting tears. "All I want is to know what happened to Mel. To be safe and for this to be over. And once it is, I can worry about whatever evidence the cops think they have. It won't stick. How could it?"

A lump filled his throat, and he pulled her close, then kissed her strawberry-scented hair. He'd worked with a lot of brave, strong women. Women with intense training and hard-fought skills learned in the field. But right then, he was certain that Jo could match them all.

When they separated, her hand went to the

doorknob. "I'm scared we're wrong," she admitted. "What if this MacGuffin isn't in the book?"

"Then we'll come up with a new plan. Find a new clue."

She hesitated, then nodded. "Right. Of course, we will." She pushed open the door and flipped on the light. The office looked as it had on Monday, but Red barely acknowledged it. Instead, he headed straight to the bookshelf and the oversized canvas-covered dictionary that he'd noticed a time or two but had never thought about.

He pulled it down, noting the weight of it. He opened the cover. Just like *Anna Karenina,* there was a metal plate inside the book with a six-digit combination code.

"Go ahead," Jo whispered.

He moved to the desk, then manipulated the lock, using the passcode from Mel's phone. He didn't expect it to work—most likely, they'd need to pry the thing open—but as soon as he turned the tiny handle, the interior lid popped up.

"Holy shit," he said as Jo gasped.

"Are those—"

"Diamonds," he said, pulling out the clear bag and testing the weight in his hand. "Three, four pounds, I'd guess. At least five-hundred carats, probably six."

"Good God, Mel. What the hell were you doing?"

"If he double-crossed someone—and it sure as hell sounds like he did—then this is one hell of a motive for murder."

"They must be worth a fortune." Both fear and awe tinged Jo's voice.

"About five million minimum retail," Red guessed. "Probably half that on the black market."

"Can they be traced?"

He put the diamonds back in the book. "No idea. Not an area I've ever worked in. But let's go see what we can find out."

Less than an hour later they were in Santa Monica at Stark Security. They'd called Ryan from the car, and now they were seated in his office as agents and staff worked in the main area.

"Thanks for meeting us," Red said. "Sorry to interrupt your day off."

"Not a problem," Ryan assured them. "I was doing some work around the house, killing time until Jamie gets home. She's been on set since four am."

"I overheard someone talking about that at Abby's shower," Jo says. "She's in a Carson Donnelly film?"

The wattage of Ryan's smile could power all of Santa Monica. "The second female lead. I'm so fucking proud of her."

"That's great," Jo says.

"It is," Ryan says. "It's also not why you're here. What's going on?"

"Two things," Red says, then tells Ryan about the cops and the life insurance.

"Hardly enough to arrest on, but who knows what else they have? If someone's setting you up," he adds, his attention on Jo, "they're probably parsing out the information slowly."

"Lucky me."

"You want us to look into it? See if we can trace the source of the policy?"

"Hell, yeah."

"Not a problem. But that's not worthy of a trip to Santa Monica. We could have set that up with a phone call. What's the bigger issue?"

"These," Red said, plunking the fake book on Ryan's desk, then opening it to reveal the diamonds, now sparkling under the fluorescent light.

"Yeah," Ryan said, his brows rising. "Definitely a conversation to be had in person." He looked between the two of them. "This is what they want, then."

"We assume so."

"Can you hold onto them?" Jo asked. "Mac-Guffin or not, I'm not comfortable carrying around millions of dollars' worth of diamonds. You must have a kickass safe here, right?"

"We do, and we can. But you're really here to see if we can trace them."

"Can you?" Red asked.

Ryan leaned back with a sigh. "Odds are slim, but there's a chance. Hang on."

He punched a button on his desk, and a moment later the new agent, Simon, came in. Red could tell the man was not only strong, but well-trained simply by the way he held himself. "What's up?"

His eyes darted to the diamonds, but to his credit, he didn't ask and his face registered no reaction at all. Red had to give the man props.

"Sorry to pull you away, but we have a quick question."

"No worries. I was about to pack it in anyway. Too many pages of useless data. I need sleep and a fresh look tomorrow."

"We won't keep you long, but unless I'm misremembering, Devlin mentioned that you participated in a couple of operations surrounding conflict diamonds."

"You know you're not misremembering, Hunter," Simon said. "I can't imagine you ever misremembering anything."

"What are conflict diamonds?" Jo asked.

"Same thing as blood diamonds," Simon told her. "Pretty much boils down to diamonds mined in a war zone to support an insurgency. A lot of people die for those diamonds," he added. "Thus the blood moniker."

"We're wondering about these," Ryan said, nodding at the diamonds. "Can we trace them to a source? Tell if they're conflict diamonds? Can we get any information about them at all?"

Simon bent for a closer look, then shook his head. "Once they're cut and polished, it's impossible to tell. But reputable diamonds will have a pedigree. Paperwork showing where they were mined, cut, polished. All that stuff. My guess? These are either conflict diamonds or stolen. If they're blood diamonds, tracing them will be next to impossible. But I have some contacts in the gemstone world. I can ask around and see if there've been any major heists in the last year or so."

"We'd appreciate it," Red said. "Especially if they have any leads on who might have pulled off such a thing."

"Not a problem." He gave them all a nod, told Ryan he'd report back, then left the office.

"Seems like a good guy," Red said.

"He is. Keeps to himself mostly, but he knows his stuff and doesn't play games." Ryan pushed back from his desk and stood. "I doubt we'll know anything today, but if we do I'll be in touch. Or just tell you at the party tonight."

"I'd lost track of the days," Jo said later as they were walking back to Red's car. "I can't believe that party is tonight. I'm so happy for Abby. And, honestly, I'm completely curious about what Damien Stark's house looks like."

"It's fabulous," Red told her. "They invited me over after the situation in New York. It's huge by my standards, but considering Stark's net worth, it's modest. I liked that about it. Felt like a home, not a showpiece."

"I heard it has an underground garage and tennis courts."

"Right on both counts."

"I would love to see him play someday. My mom was a fan back in the day and I can remember watching him. I think she had a crush on him, even though he was so young. Like what, seventeen or something? I know I had a crush."

Red laughed. "Should I be jealous?"

"Nope," she said, laughing. "Not in the least."

"At any rate," he said once they were walking again, "it's nice but at the end of the day, it's just a house."

"Like you're just a guy?"

"I am."

She tugged him to a stop and kissed him, a hot deep kiss that earned them more than a few catcalls from passersby.

"You're not," she said, when she pulled away. She started to walk again, but he pulled her back.

"I'm sorry."

"For what?" she asked.

He hesitated, trying to put it into words. "For being so fucked up. For not telling you years ago how much I wanted you. And for feeling guilty about wanting you in the first place. You belonged to Mel, and I loved him, and I hated myself for craving you."

"Don't," she said. "Don't feel sorry about the past. We have each other now, and we've already agreed that Mel would be happy for us."

"I love you, Jo."

Her easy smile warmed him like the sunshine. "Good. Because I love you, too." She bit her lower lip, then tilted her head, her eyes dancing. "Do you know what you can be sorry for?"

"What?"

She slid into his arms, then cupped his cock, clearly uninterested in whether anyone was watching. "For making me late for the party."

CHAPTER TWENTY-THREE

By the time we need to get dressed for the party, I'm desperately on edge and begging for Red to please, please let me come again. And he, damn him, isn't agreeable at all.

After three mind-blowing orgasms, I probably shouldn't care, but he's played me like a symphony all afternoon, building the music of my passion up and up into a series of ever increasing explosions until I'm begging for more and more and more.

Now my body is hot and needy, my pussy aching for him, and every touch to my clit sends waves of pleasure through me. Waves that suggest a coming tsunami—one that Red is very firmly denying me.

"Please," I murmur.

"We need to get ready," he says, sounding all too smug.

I squeeze my legs together, but to no avail. Right now, I'm on my knees, my chest against the mattress and my wrists bound to the headboard. My ass is in the air, and my thighs are spread. I can still feel the lingering sting of Red's palm against my rear, and when I close my eyes I can remember the way that sweet sting curled through me, seeming to center at my core.

He brought me so close like that, then fucked me from behind, one hand teasing my clit and the other around my neck as he took me so hard the bed pounded against the wall, actually shaking one of my small, framed photos free.

Each time I'd exploded around him, and each time he'd taken me further, whispering naughty words and telling me all the ways he intended to use me when we returned that night. How he'd tie my hands behind my back and hold my head while I sucked him off. How he'd ease me into a hot tub and gently wash me. How he'd blindfold me, then sit across the room, watching as I got myself off.

And oh, God, I want it all.

Right now, though, I just want him to make me come again. Just once more to release the ache in my pussy. And since he's refused, I'll just have to take care of that myself. I push back my knees so that I'm flat on the bed, then undulate my hips, trying to use the friction of the bed to make me come.

Red chuckles. "Would you like to tell me what you're doing?"

"Getting off," I say. "Or trying to."

The smack across my ass is sweetly delicious— but it doesn't take me over.

"Behave or we'll miss the party," he says, knowing full well that if anything can control me, that threat can. No way am I missing Abby and Renly's send-off on their honeymoon. He moves to the head of the bed and unties my wrists. "Get dressed," he orders. "But no underwear."

I slide into his arms. "Yes, *sir*," I say, then kiss him. "By the way, I like you bossy."

I can tell he's trying not to, but he laughs, then smacks my ass as I dance away to my bedroom so that I can grab a shower and raid my closet.

When I come back, he's already dressed, looking sexier than sin in a gray suit and a maroon tie. I'm in an ankle-length dress with a fitted bodice and a flowing skirt. Not formal attire, but definitely fancy.

I slide into his arms and accept his kiss. "You look gorgeous," he says.

"Back at you." I fiddle with his tie, as if straightening it even though it's already perfect, simply for the pleasure of feeling domestic with this man.

Then I step back and look him up and down for so long that he finally narrows his eyes and says, "What?"

"I'm not sure how to say it," I tell him.

"That doesn't sound good."

I laugh. "No, it's very good." I step back, then reach for his hands. "Do you have any idea how incredible you make me feel? I don't mean in general—I've known for years that being around you lights me up. I mean in bed." I swallow, feeling bold for talking about it so openly. "For what you do to me. What you make me do. And all the rest still to come."

His mouth curves up as I speak, and now it's a full-blown smile. "Well, that makes two of us."

I smirk. "Yeah, well here's the thing. I think this is who you are. Who you always have been." He starts to pull away, but I tighten my grip on his hands. "I know they hurt you. I know she tortured you. But I think part of the torture was them stealing control. You've always been a man who needs it. After that, I think that need just rose to the forefront."

"Jo—"

"I'm not saying that's good or bad. I'm just saying that I don't think you're as broken as you believe you are or that your shrinks have said you are. Maybe you thought it was wrong to want what you do, but it's not. And, yeah, the torture was real, that's for damn sure." I press my hand to his heart. "But the control you crave in here? I think you've always had that. I think after *they* controlled *you*,

you let yourself think that need was vile. But it's not. I promise you it's not."

I bite my lip, studying his face as I wonder if I've said too much or if I'm so off-base he's going to close up on me. But he's watching me and I can almost see the thoughts playing on his face, as if maybe there's something real and solid in my words.

"I think maybe you survived *because* you had this core ability to hold onto that control and wait for your opportunity. You're saying she did this to you, but how dare you give her credit for something so inherently you. Don't you get it, Red? She didn't make you who you are—but it's because of who you are that you ultimately ended the bitch."

He says nothing, but I see the tension in his cheek, as if he's holding back deep emotion.

I lick my lips, suddenly unsure if I've overstepped. "Red," I begin. "I'm sorry if—"

I don't have the chance to finish the sentence, because he pulls me to him, then closes his mouth over mine. The kiss is long and deep, and I'm light-headed when he releases me.

"Does that mean you think I'm right?" I ask.

"I don't know," he says. "Honestly, I'm not even sure it matters anymore. All I know is that I love you."

I love you.

Red's words still fill my heart an hour later when we're in the car and heading toward Malibu. He's said it before, of course, but this time was different somehow on the heels of my amateur analysis of what makes him tick. What he needs.

It's what I need, too, and that's something I hadn't realized until we fully opened up to each other. He's been my best friend for about half my life. Now, he's so much more.

"What?" he asks, flashing me a grin as he glances sideways at me.

"Just thinking about how happy I am. We're chasing a killer who's using us to find a stash of diamonds, our lives are in danger, and the cops think I killed my husband who was one of my best friends. And despite all of that, I've never been happier."

He takes my hand. "Oh, baby. Me, too. And when this is over…"

"What?" I urge.

"I haven't decided. But we're going away somewhere, just us. Someplace where I can take you out at night and show you off. Someplace with the kind of clubs that require secret passwords. Someplace with fancy hotels where I can keep you all to myself. We're going to make up for lost time, Jo." He raises his brows, his lips twitching as he adds, "I hope you have the stamina."

I laugh. "Try me."

"Oh, believe me, I intend to."

I'm about to say he can pull over and try to tire me out right there by the side of this empty Malibu side road when his phone rings, the display showing that it's Mario.

"Got news?" Red asks in lieu of a hello.

"The news is that I'm a bona fide genius," Mario says. "We couldn't clean up that reflection at all, and nothing else was popping from the interior security cams. Caught her a couple of times, but always with her head down. Woman was careful, I'll give her that. But I figured there must have been a time they were seen together outside, even if they were being careful. So I've had a team scouring CCTV footage from an ATM across the street. And bingo, bingo, we won the freaking lottery."

"How so?" I ask.

"She had her head down there, too, but there was a wreck not that long ago. Someone smashed full-speed into someone else. And when they did, our gal reacted. Lifted her head. Put it down fast again, but we managed to capture a freeze frame. And it's a pretty damn clean image. Enough that we can start running it through the system."

"Send it," Red says, something harsh and unfamiliar in his voice. He maneuvers the car onto the shoulder, then kills the engine. "I need to see her face."

"Red, you know it can't possibly be—," I begin but he shoots me such a hard, bitter look, that I silence myself. He'll know I'm right soon enough. He told me how she died in the explosion. Whoever this woman is, I'm certain she's not a ghost.

"Sending now," Mario says, this time shooting it to Red's phone since I hadn't shoved my tablet into my tiny cocktail bag.

I watch as Red opens the file, and my heart flips I see his face go completely pale.

It is her. Somehow it's the woman. His tormentor. The bitch who tried to break him.

And, as I watch the horror spread over his face, I wonder if this time she's managed to do exactly that.

CHAPTER TWENTY-FOUR

"She's alive. How the hell is she alive?"

He'd voiced the question aloud, but it didn't sound like his voice. Hell, this didn't feel like his life. How could any of this be real?

"She?" Mario's voice startles him from his thoughts. "You know this woman?"

"Yes," Jo begins. "She's—"

But he didn't let her finish. He reached over and disconnected the call. "This isn't happening."

"Yes," Jo said, "it is. Red, look at me. You can handle this. You're strong enough to handle anything."

"I need to think. We're almost to Stark's. I'll drop you there. You'll want to see Abby." His voice sounded dead, but it didn't matter. He just had to make it through this second, then this minute, then this hour. Do that, and maybe he could think clearly. Could come up with a plan. Could figure out what had gone wrong. How she'd survived.

And what the fuck she wanted with him now.

He sank back in the driver's seat, realization hitting him with the force of a sledgehammer and shattering his heart to pieces.

"This is about me. All of it. Mel's death. Your attack. This bullshit race to find the diamonds. Even his affair. It's all about me." He turned in the seat to meet Jo's eyes, knowing she must despise him for this. "She came for me. She's playing cat and mouse, and everyone I care about has been ensnared in her trap." His heart pounded in his chest as bile rose in his throat. *Oh, God. He was going to be sick.*

"Red, *no*. This isn't your fault. None of it."

"The hell it isn't. You think this isn't about me, then you're—"

"Of course, it's about you," she snapped, the severity of her words hitting him with the force of a slap. "You're right. I have absolutely no doubt that you're right, and it's fucking terrifying. She survived, I get that. Somehow that bitch survived and somehow she found you. She played you. She seduced Mel. She probably planted the diamonds. She's trying to hurt you, and the odds are pretty damn good she wants to hurt me, too."

She exhaled, her shaky breath the only visible

clue to her fear. "But none of that is your fault, Red. Not one single bit of it."

"The hell it's not. Back then I should have—"

"What? You should have been an action hero? You're not starring in a Marvel movie. They drugged you, they tortured you, and from what you told me they had you tied down pretty damn good. So you tell me, Red. How the hell was that your fault?"

Her eyes flashed with anger and frustration, and oh, how he understood it. He knew she was right—every iota of common sense in his body agreed with her. And yet there was still that mantra —*if he'd only had a knife back then, even the shortest of blades.*

Things were different now.

He steeled himself, reaching out to grip the steering wheel, tension running through his arms, his hands so tight his knuckles were white. He saw the tendons pop in his arms, the muscles rippling from years of working out, of ensuring he'd never be a victim again, the scars that stood out as reminders of what he'd endured—and that in the future, he could prevail.

Would prevail.

He could handle this. He was prepared for this. Hell, he had to be.

"Dammit, Red, talk to me. Don't you dare pull

away from me because this bitch is back in your life..."

He turned to her, the words and her tone finally getting through to him. "Jo—oh, God, Jo—no. Never. Christ, don't you know how much I need you?"

The relief in her eyes filled his heart and fueled his determination. And, yes, he did need her. Needed the feel of her, the taste of her. Need to touch her and let the knowledge of what he was fighting for fill him. Because the fight was coming—he was damn sure of that.

Without any thought about what he was doing, he pulled her toward him. She came willingly, neither of them worrying about that damn dress as she clambered over the center console to straddle his lap. "I need you," he said, his fingers thrusting inside her as she frantically worked at his fly.

"Yes, yes," she murmured, abandoning her task as his fingers filled her and she arched back, riding his hand. "Oh, God, Red, I'd thought—"

"No. No, just come for me. Not another word until I feel you explode."

Kaplow!

The window shattered, sending bits of safety glass flying everywhere. Immediately, he pushed Jo off him and down onto the passenger seat, then covered her with his body.

"Get out of the car," a male voice said from

behind them. "Get out now," a second voice added, "or you watch the bitch die."

"They're going to take us both," Red whispered to her.

"I know." He heard the fear, and the courage in her reply.

He started to rise, lifting his hands as he did, and knowing full well that, at least at the moment, there wasn't a damn thing else he could do. Especially now that he could see the two laser sights—both aimed at Jo's chest. "I'll get us out of this," he promised. "Somehow, I'll get us out."

"I believe you," she said.

Then something hard and heavy impacted the back of his head. He heard the sharp blast of Jo's scream.

And then the world went black.

CHAPTER TWENTY-FIVE

I wake in a darkness so thick I almost fear that they've blinded me. I'm naked, huddled in a corner, rough stone under my thighs and behind my back.

I'm shivering, but not from cold. The room is stifling, warm and humid with stale, thick air. But from the way I'm shaking, I might as well be on an ice floe.

"Red?" My voice is hoarse and I try to swallow, but there's no moisture in my mouth at all. "Red, are you here?"

Silence.

I reach out, crawling to my left, away from the stone wall to my right. But I barely go a foot before hitting another wall. Then another. It's a box. A small stone box. A miniature prison, like a dollhouse for the damned.

And I'm in here all alone.

"Red," I whisper, my eyes too dry to shed tears. "Please be safe. Please, please be alive."

I pull my knees up and hug them to my chest, telling myself I have to think logically. I have to figure out what happened. I have to try to find some advantage, though God knows what that could be.

Think, dammit. What do you know? What can you do?

The *do* part of that equation is pretty minimal. I have no weapons, no clothes, no idea where I am, where Red is, or how to get out of this room.

Trapped. I'm trapped.

I squeeze my hands tight and close my eyes, telling myself to calm down. There's no real point in closing my eyes, but at least this way, it's supposed to be dark.

"It can't have been that long," I say. "And they want something. If they'd just wanted me dead, they would have killed me in the car."

The car. I realize with a start that until that moment, I'd remembered nothing from before. I'd simply been *here*, alone without Red. But I didn't remember how that had come to pass. Didn't even realize the memory was missing.

But it floods back now. The feel of him as I straddled him in the car. His horror that the woman who'd tormented him for so many months was alive. That she'd been playing cat and mouse with us.

That she'd sent men to bring us in.

I hear a pitiful sound, and realize it's coming from me. I'm seeing those laser sights again, feeling the rough hands on my arms hauling me out of Red's car, the ache in my throat as I scream his name, the bile that rises as Red slumps to the ground, a man in black with aviator glasses sneering at his inert form.

I screamed and fought, but it didn't matter. All it took was one fist against my jaw. I tasted blood. My head hit the pavement.

And then I woke up in the dark.

But it hasn't been that long.

I think about that, wondering how I know that. I'm not hungry, but that could be because of fear. But I don't think so. I think it's only been a few hours. And if that's true, the maybe, surely, Red is still alive.

Surely, I'll see him again.

I shiver, the possibility that I won't too horrible to contemplate.

I hug myself, trying to organize my thoughts, but to what end? I have neither skills nor opportunity. I'm in a box. I'm in a coffin.

I start to shake, fear settling deep in my bones.

"*Stop it,*" I say. "*It's going to be fine. Red will make it fine.*"

"Oh, I sincerely doubt that." The woman's voice is low and melodic with an accent I can't place. It seems to surround me, and I can't tell if she's in front of me, behind, or above.

Above? Am I in a pit?

I look up, and I think that maybe—possibly—I see a glimmer of light. And then, as I blink and my eyes adjust, I know that I'm right. About the light and about the pit. Because that's where I am, and someone is opening it from the top and light is seeping in, and then, suddenly, I'm blinking at white, blinding light.

I cringe and throw my arm over my eye, then tumble backward when someone slams me in the chest with some sort of prod.

I cry out and scurry backward, my eyes adjusting to see that one of the walls has swung away like a door, and two men dressed entirely in black stand behind a woman in a black suit skirt and a silk tank, her stiletto heels little more than nail points on the stone floor.

"Where's Red? What have you done with him?"

"You will find out soon enough, Josephine," she says in that same accent. "But first, I should introduce myself. I'm the bitch who's going to torture the man you're fucking, you naughty little whore. And do you know how I will do this thing? Hmm?"

I can't answer. My throat is too tight, and I feel like I'm strangling on unshed tears.

"No? Well, then I shall tell you, yes? It is so very clever. Because, you see, he loves you, no? And so I shall do the best torture. One that will surely destroy him. I will let him watch, helpless, as you die."

CHAPTER TWENTY-SIX

Red slammed into consciousness, jarred back to reality by the force of the water sprayed in his face. He sputtered, his soaked shirt sticking to his chest as he tried to move, tried to remember.

Then he saw *her* and everything clicked back into place. He tried to surge forward but was foiled by the chair to which he was strapped, one thick rope around his chest that bound him to the back. His arms were crossed behind him and tied together above the wrist. His legs weren't bound, but all that allowed was for him to bounce across the floor, and she'd undoubtedly kill him while he tried to move.

Just like before. Dear God, this was just like before.

Except it wasn't. This time he had his legs, if he

could manage to time the use of them. That was a benefit.

But they also had Jo unless—*please, no*—they'd already killed her. And having her in their custody changed everything. He might take a risk with his own life, but not with hers.

"Where is she?"

"Your sweet Lisa? Those other bitches? Why they're dead, of course."

He growled, the rising sound low and coming out like an animal about to attack. He lunged forward, but all that happened was the chair tipped a bit, then righted.

But that movement—that slight movement—cut through the haze in his brain. *He would get free. He had to. Jo needed him, and there was no way in hell he was letting her down.*

"Oh, did you mean the lovely Josephine? Why she's fine as well. Naked and ready for you." She smiled, then settled into the empty chair behind which she'd been standing. "I'm so looking forward to watching."

His entire being screamed for him to attack, but he forced himself to focus. To study his surroundings. To think. To analyze. To plan.

Cinderblock walls. Three hanging bulbs for lighting. A small room, probably ten by twelve, with one metal door on the far side. Two men guarding it. No windows that he could see. They were in a basement, perhaps.

"I killed you once already," he snarled. "This time, I'll do a better job."

Her laugh was full of delight, a sweet sound in utter contrast with the foul, sadistic bitch he knew her to be.

"You didn't kill me." She stood, then crossed to him. She bent over, putting her hands on the armrests as she got right in his face. "But I will kill you."

Fear spiked, panic building. Every flashback he'd had throughout the years threatening to come back. To fill his head, debilitating him. Making him useless to himself. And, oh please no, to Jo.

No. Goddamit, no.

He'd survived this bitch before, and he could damn well do it again. He had to.

"It won't be an easy death, Mr. Cooper," she said, her eyes dipping to the hose on the floor. He noticed that there was no barrel in which to submerge him, thank God, but he could see that the hose was the high-pressure kind used by firemen. She'd awakened him with it, but not at full pressure, he was sure of that.

At full force, she could drown him simply by holding it steady long enough.

A smile flickered on her lips. "Oh, no. No my dear Mr. Cooper. You will not die as easily as that.

Not right away, at least. First you will watch another woman you care about die. As I had to watch my husband die after you buried us in rubble."

"No more than you or he deserved," he snarled, fury that she'd dare hurt Jo coiling through him.

"Try to be nicer, Mr. Cooper. It won't save your woman, but it might earn you a quick death when you follow her. Right now, I am looking forward to killing you slowly. Painfully. But if you use your manners and show me your remorse for killing Lars, then perhaps I shall show the tiniest bit of mercy, no?"

His lip curled up, but he stayed silent. The bitch was insane, and he wasn't going to rile her. Not because he cared what she did to him, but if he pissed her off too much, she'd undoubtedly take it out on Jo.

Think, dammit. *A plan. A strategy.* When his opportunity came—and, oh, he knew damn well it would come, he had to be ready. Had to be poised to kill the bitch in an instant, then go after her two protectors.

And then he had to find Jo.

He drew in a breath, then another, trying to relax his body. To ready himself for any opportunity. Behind his back, he tugged at his wrists, trying to no avail to loosen the ropes. He switched tactics, instead closing his hands over his opposite forearms, then breathing in when he felt the scar tissue beneath his fingers. The touch calmed him, reminding him that he could do this. He had the skill, the power. All he needed was an opportunity.

She tilted her head, clearly giving a silent order to one of the men, who pushed the metal door open and disappeared. "You should rejoice, Mr. Cooper. Soon you will see your love. Enjoy the moment, as you will soon lose her as well. Though do not worry. There will be time enough. I assure you, her death will be slow."

"How the fuck did you survive?"

Her beautiful face contorted. "Against the odds, Mr. Cooper. And every moment I was trapped with my dead lover, I thought of you. I planned my revenge. And I waited for the opportunity."

"You planned all of this. Mel's death. The diamonds." He hoped the words kept her distracted. At this point, he didn't give a fuck how she'd pulled this off. All he cared about was slicing the bitch's throat.

Behind his back, he beat the knuckle of each thumb against the scar tissue on his arms, hoping against hope that he could find the pressure point. That his fucked up plan would work, because God knew it wasn't anything he'd ever had the opportunity to test.

"Of course I did. Mel Cooper was an easy

mark. So bored in his marriage. So ready for glamour and passion."

"I'll never believe Mel would help smuggle or sell stolen diamonds. The only thing that surprises me is that you managed to pretend to be a woman decent enough to attract his attention."

He forced his voice to stay level, hoping she'd assume the tightness and deep breaths he couldn't avoid were a result of fear and anger, and not what he was doing behind his back.

Because now he had the knife.

One of two he'd had surgically implanted by the SOC's chief surgeon after Seagrave gave him permission for the procedure. A design he'd come up with himself, then refined over a course of meetings with Dr. Hargrove. She'd been hesitant at first, but had agreed that the concept had utility. And if Red had wanted to be a guinea pig, then so be it.

Now, he could report back that the system worked. The applied pressure on his arm in just the right place had send the titanium blade forward at an angle, slicing up through the scar tissue. His curled fingers had made contact, and despite the slickness from the blood, he'd been able to grab the textured handle that had been scored for traction to ameliorate the risk of dropping the weapon in a situation exactly like this.

He hoped to hell there wasn't much blood dripping on to the floor behind him as he strained to twist his hand and went to work on the ropes, even as his other thumb worked to release the blade hidden in his left forearm.

Each knife was only barely over four inches long, handle included, but it was something. More than something since he'd been training constantly with similar short blades since the week after he underwent the procedure. Blade work, martial arts, weight training. He'd never given it up; he'd kept in shape. He'd been preparing for a day like this.

"And here is your beloved," the woman said, her voice still smug enough that Red was confident she didn't know that his right arm was almost free.

He looked up, all of his pleasure at almost being free of the chair fading when he saw Jo. She was naked, her hands bound behind her as she half-stumbled into the room as the man dragged her toward a chair.

But the worst of it was when she whispered, "I love you."

"Jo—oh, God, Jo. I will get you out of here," he said as the last strand of rope binding his wrists snapped. "I swear it."

The woman laughed, but Jo whispered "I know." She was about to say something else, but the man landed a hard punch against her jaw.

When she lifted her head again, he saw the blood flow from the gash in her lip.

"Leave her the fuck alone."

"No," the woman said. "I think better to let her die slowly, as she already is. Boris, show our guest."

The second man at the door—Boris, apparently —went to Jo, then released her hands. Then fell to her sides as she sat in the chair, pale and terrified. And with blood dripping from the slits on her wrists.

"You bitch," he snarled. "I swear, I will fucking kill you."

"No," the woman said, moving closer to him, taunting him from less than a foot away. "You are helpless. And I shall enjoy spending this last bit of time together as she dies. And then, my dear Mr. Cooper, I'll cut off your balls and leave you to bleed out, too. You see how I am kind after all? You will be following your whore into hell."

The watch she wore emitted a short *ping*, and she glanced at it, frowning. "Tomas, go check the perimeter."

The first man gave a quick nod, then left, leaving behind one hell of an opportunity.

Red hadn't managed to release the left knife yet, but he also knew he might not get a better chance. With this back still strapped to the chair, he lunged up and around, using the chair legs to knock the bitch off balance. At the same time, he aimed the knife, hoping against hope that the hours of training paid off.

He let the knife fly, gratified when it lodged in

Boris's throat. To her credit, Jo lunged sideways, knocking the chair over as she lifted her arms and clutched her wrists, positioned now to staunch the flow of blood.

He wanted to go her, but the bitch was climbing back to her feet. Red spun again, but she jumped clear of the chair legs. His arm was unbound, but he hadn't yet managed to free the second knife. Now, as the bitch burst toward him, howling obscenities, he slammed the side of his right hand down on the spring, releasing the knife with a burst of sharp, fresh pain.

He relished it. Let it fuel him as he rounded on her, sending her and him and the chair tumbling. He slit her throat, one quick slice, and then to be sure, he lifted his body and then chair, then slammed it down hard on her chest.

The bitch was dead.

He used the knife to cut his back free, then scrambled to stand, blood dripping from his arms.

A few feet from Jo, Boris had dislodged the knife and, gasping, was crawling to Jo who was trying to push herself away.

"Jo! No. Stay still. Don't increase your heart rate."

Boris lifted his head, sneered, then fell silent when Red kicked the knife from his hand before reaching down and snapping the bastard's neck. He grabbed the man's pistol and tucked it in the waist-band of his slacks.

Then he ripped off his shirt and used one of the knives to slice off the hem to bind Jo's hands before cutting her loose and helping her to her feet. Tenderly, he put the now-mangled shirt over her head and helped her into it.

"I never doubted," she whispered, and oh, God, how he loved her.

"We have to go. The other one's still out there, and he may have gone to meet more of them."

She nodded. "I can walk. I'm woozy, but I can manage."

"I've got you," he said, his hand on her arm. "And I'm never letting go."

"I know. Let's get out of here. Please."

They moved as quickly as they could, checking corners, trying to find their way out of the under-ground maze. Then they turned into a corridor, only to be confronted by Tomas stepping from a shadow.

Red shoved Jo behind him, then shifted his weapons, a knife in each hand.

He felt the tug as Jo pulled the gun from his waistband, then heard the click as she fired. Except nothing happened. The gun was completely empty.

"I assure you my weapon is not," Tomas said. "And I will relish—"

He didn't finish the sentence. As he spoke, Red released one knife, sending it hurling straight into Tomas's eye. It made contact a split second before the man's head exploded, sending Red stumbling backward in surprise and confusion as he pulled Jo to the ground, covering her.

Then his mind cleared as everything clicked into place. As he saw Simon standing behind Tomas, his weapon drawn, Quincy backing him up.

He closed his eyes and drew a breath, then opened them again when he heard the distinct foot-falls of someone running toward them. Renly burst around the corner, Emma right beside him.

"Oh, thank God," Renly said. "Christ, man, what happened?"

"I ran into an old friend," Red said. "But it's all good now." He helped Jo up, they clung to each other. "I'd say it's all just about perfect."

———

"Just another hour, and then you're free to go," the doctor said, adjusting something on Jo's IV. They were in the Stark Security infirmary, and she was being treated by the physician on call.

"I'll be happy to get unhooked," Jo said.

"But she's fine?" Red asked. "You're sure?"

"I am," the doctor said. "You'll both heal nicely."

Red nodded, glancing down at his bandaged forearms. The knives were gone, but first chance he had, he was having Dr. Hargrove redo the procedure. With luck, he'd never have to use them again, but he wasn't taking chances.

Red looked over to where Renly leaned against the doorjamb. The others were nearby, too, he knew, but were kindly giving them space. "Sorry about your party, bro. But thanks for the calvary."

Renly chuckled. "Yeah, I hate it when rabid human traffickers ruin my soirees. Looks so bad on the social register."

"How did you find us?" Jo asked.

Red had already heard the story, but she'd passed out in the car and missed it, so he let Renly tell her again.

"Quincy saw Red's car on the road and reported in. That's when Mario shared the picture he'd sent you, and Simon recognized the woman."

"Simon did?" Jo looked to Red, who nodded and took up the story.

"Apparently she's the head of the trafficking cell he's been chasing. Says he and Devlin Saint owes us big time."

"So this was about trafficking?"

"No," Red said. "It was about me. She tracked me down. Wanted revenge for her husband. I thought they'd both died, turns out she escaped and this whole thing was a cat and mouse game with our lives, just like we thought. All of it was fake. She arranged for the life insurance. Planted the diamonds. All of it except Mel's affair, but I'm sure she pushed hard on that front, worked to seduce him. He loved you, Jo. He would never have hurt you."

"I know," she said, then reached for him. "Where were we? And how did you guys find us?"

"Abandoned factory," Renly said. "And you owe Mario for getting us there. Simon had some ideas about the general vicinity, but what led us to you was Mario's tech. He put a tracker in Mel's phone and the clones, and Red had it in his pocket."

"Why?" Jo asked.

Renly shrugged. "I asked Mario that. Said he thought it seemed like a good idea."

"Can't argue with that," Red said.

"I'm going to get out of your hair. Abby wants to see you before we head off on the honeymoon, so we'll stick around until you're released."

"Thanks, bro," Red said, reaching for his brother's hand.

"Anytime. For that matter, why not take Damien up on his offer and we can watch each other's backs regularly."

"We'll see," Red said, not ready to admit that he'd already been thinking along those lines. Part time, maybe. He had a distillery to run after all. And years of catching up to do with Jo.

When they were alone, Jo smiled at him. "I never doubted you'd get us out."

He made a scoffing sound. "Not a sound bet. I'd failed once before, remember."

Her grin made his heart sing. "I knew, though." She squeezed his hand. "I love you, Red," she said, and he knew that he would never tire of hearing those words. "I've loved you for a very long time."

"Oh, baby. Me too."

"We both made wrong turns. But somehow we ended up exactly where we're supposed to be."

"That's true. And my first mistake was not grabbing you when I had the chance. But you're mine now," he told her. "And I'm never going to let you go."

EPILOGUE

One year later

I stand in the surf, Red right beside me, looking out at the Pacific as I hold the urn with my first husband's ashes.

We're at The Resort at Cortez for a weekend retreat for all Stark Security personnel and their spouses or significant others. I'm here with Red, of course, even though the boat ride did a number on my first trimester nausea.

"Sorry that took so long," he calls from across the beach. He's heading toward me from Damien's bungalow where he's just finished a quick call with a client about a recent operation. He hurries barefoot across the sand to my side.

I smile in greeting. "No problem. I was just

thinking about what a long road it's been, and yet I can't imagine any other one."

He pulls me close, then kisses my forehead. "You okay?"

"I am. It's not Catalina, but I think he'd love this place." In college, we three used to go to Catalina Island at least once a month to eat, drink, and laze on the beach.

"We're here now more often, too," Red says. "This way, he's close to us."

I nod, then take the lid off the urn where we've kept Mel's ashes since his memorial last year.

"Ready?"

Red nods. "Love you, buddy," he says. "And next year we're celebrating the release of Mel's Special Reserve. Try not to let it go to your head. We love you. And we know wherever you are, you're watching out for both of us."

It's my turn, and I blink back tears. "We miss you, Mel. Friend. Husband. I hope you know how much I've always loved you. You and Red were the best friends I ever had. Despite everything, we had a good life. I hope you thought so, too."

Since it's heavy, I give Red the urn, afraid I might drop it. We stand with the wind behind us, and as he tilts it, I watch Mel's ashes catch in the wind and get blown out to the sea.

"Goodbye," I whisper when the urn is empty.

"Slange, buddy," Red says, and I smile at the

toast. With a sigh, I press my hand over my belly where little Mel or Melanie is growing, then fall in step beside my husband as we head back toward the bungalows.

Renly is there, standing with Abby. A few feet behind them, Simon is arguing with Damien, though I can't tell about what.

Abby gives me a hug and Renly hooks an arm around Red. "You two good?" he asks.

"We're fine," Red says after catching my eye. "But what's the story with Simon?"

Though he still does the occasional job with Devlin Saint, Simon has signed on officially with Stark Security, so I'm assuming something's up with one of his operations.

"More like he's trying to avoid an operation in the first place," Renly says when I suggest as much.

"What do you mean?"

Renly and Abby share amused glances. "You know how much love Simon doesn't have for the Hollywood elite?"

"Sure." I don't know Simon that well, but his dislike of the Hollywood A-list is hard to miss.

"So what's happened?" Red asks.

"Francesca Muratti happened," Abby says, her lips twitching. "Apparently she just hired the agency. And our man Simon is the guy on point."

THE END

I hope you enjoyed Jo and Red's story! Be sure not to miss **Simon and Francesca** in *Charmed By You*, coming August 9 from 1001 Dark Nights. Visit www.juliekenner.com to subscribe to my newsletter and be notified as soon as it's available for preorder!

Did you miss **Renly's story**? You can find it in *Memories of You*. Wondering about **Red's hostage experience with Damien**? Be sure to read *Cherish Me*.

XXOO

J. Kenner
xxoo

MEET DAMIEN STARK

Only his passion could set her free...

Meet Damien Stark in Release Me, *book 1 of the wildly sensual series that's left millions of readers breathless ...*

Chapter One

A cool ocean breeze caresses my bare shoulders, and I shiver, wishing I'd taken my roommate's advice and brought a shawl with me tonight. I arrived in Los Angeles only four days ago, and I haven't yet adjusted to the concept of summer temperatures changing with the setting of the sun. In Dallas, June is hot, July is hotter, and August is hell.

Not so in California, at least not by the beach.

LA Lesson Number One: Always carry a sweater if you'll be out after dark.

Of course, I could leave the balcony and go back inside to the party. Mingle with the millionaires. Chat up the celebrities. Gaze dutifully at the paintings. It is a gala art opening, after all, and my boss brought me here to meet and greet and charm and chat. Not to lust over the panorama that is coming alive in front of me. Bloodred clouds bursting against the pale orange sky. Blue-gray waves shimmering with dappled gold.

I press my hands against the balcony rail and lean forward, drawn to the intense, unreachable beauty of the setting sun. I regret that I didn't bring the battered Nikon I've had since high school. Not that it would have fit in my itty-bitty beaded purse. And a bulky camera bag paired with a little black dress is a big, fat fashion no-no.

But this is my very first Pacific Ocean sunset, and I'm determined to document the moment. I pull out my iPhone and snap a picture.

"Almost makes the paintings inside seem redundant, doesn't it?" I recognize the throaty, feminine voice and turn to face Evelyn Dodge, retired actress turned agent turned patron of the arts—and my hostess for the evening.

"I'm so sorry. I know I must look like a giddy tourist, but we don't have sunsets like this in Dallas."

"Don't apologize," she says. "I pay for that view every month when I write the mortgage check. It damn well better be spectacular."

I laugh, immediately more at ease.

"Hiding out?"

"Excuse me?"

"You're Carl's new assistant, right?" she asks, referring to my boss of three days.

"Nikki Fairchild."

"I remember now. Nikki from Texas." She looks me up and down, and I wonder if she's disappointed that I don't have big hair and cowboy boots. "So who does he want you to charm?"

"Charm?" I repeat, as if I don't know exactly what she means.

She cocks a single brow. "Honey, the man would rather walk on burning coals than come to an art show. He's fishing for investors and you're the bait." She makes a rough noise in the back of her throat. "Don't worry. I won't press you to tell me who. And I don't blame you for hiding out. Carl's brilliant, but he's a bit of a prick."

"It's the brilliant part I signed on for," I say, and she barks out a laugh.

The truth is that she's right about me being the bait. "Wear a cocktail dress," Carl had said. "Something flirty."

Seriously? I mean, *Seriously?*

I should have told him to wear his own damn

cocktail dress. But I didn't. Because I want this job. I fought to get this job. Carl's company, C-Squared Technologies, successfully launched three web-based products in the last eighteen months. That track record had caught the industry's eye, and Carl had been hailed as a man to watch.

More important from my perspective, that meant he was a man to learn from, and I'd prepared for the job interview with an intensity bordering on obsession. Landing the position had been a huge coup for me. So what if he wanted me to wear something flirty? It was a small price to pay.

Shit.

"I need to get back to being the bait," I say.

"Oh, hell. Now I've gone and made you feel either guilty or self-conscious. Don't be. Let them get liquored up in there first. You catch more flies with alcohol anyway. Trust me. I know."

She's holding a pack of cigarettes, and now she taps one out, then extends the pack to me. I shake my head. I love the smell of tobacco—it reminds me of my grandfather—but actually inhaling the smoke does nothing for me.

"I'm too old and set in my ways to quit," she says. "But God forbid I smoke in my own damn house. I swear, the mob would burn me in effigy. You're not going to start lecturing me on the dangers of secondhand smoke, are you?"

"No," I promise.

"Then how about a light?"

I hold up the itty-bitty purse. "One lipstick, a credit card, my driver's license, and my phone."

"No condom?"

"I didn't think it was that kind of party," I say dryly.

"I knew I liked you." She glances around the balcony. "What the hell kind of party am I throwing if I don't even have one goddamn candle on one goddamn table? Well, fuck it." She puts the unlit cigarette to her mouth and inhales, her eyes closed and her expression rapturous. I can't help but like her. She wears hardly any makeup, in stark contrast to all the other women here tonight, myself included, and her dress is more of a caftan, the batik pattern as interesting as the woman herself.

She's what my mother would call a brassy broad—loud, large, opinionated, and self-confident. My mother would hate her. I think she's awesome.

She drops the unlit cigarette onto the tile and grinds it with the toe of her shoe. Then she signals to one of the catering staff, a girl dressed all in black and carrying a tray of champagne glasses.

The girl fumbles for a minute with the sliding door that opens onto the balcony, and I imagine those flutes tumbling off, breaking against the hard tile, the scattered shards glittering like a wash of diamonds.

I picture myself bending to snatch up a broken

stem. I see the raw edge cutting into the soft flesh at the base of my thumb as I squeeze. I watch myself clutching it tighter, drawing strength from the pain, the way some people might try to extract luck from a rabbit's foot.

The fantasy blurs with memory, jarring me with its potency. It's fast and powerful, and a little disturbing because I haven't needed the pain in a long time, and I don't understand why I'm thinking about it now, when I feel steady and in control.

I am fine, I think. *I am fine, I am fine, I am fine.*

"Take one, honey," Evelyn says easily, holding a flute out to me.

I hesitate, searching her face for signs that my mask has slipped and she's caught a glimpse of my rawness. But her face is clear and genial.

"No, don't you argue," she adds, misinterpreting my hesitation. "I bought a dozen cases and I hate to see good alcohol go to waste. Hell no," she adds when the girl tries to hand her a flute. "I hate the stuff. Get me a vodka. Straight up. Chilled. Four olives. Hurry up, now. Do you want me to dry up like a leaf and float away?"

The girl shakes her head, looking a bit like a twitchy, frightened rabbit. Possibly one that had sacrificed his foot for someone else's good luck.

Evelyn's attention returns to me. "So how do you like LA? What have you seen? Where have you been? Have you bought a map of the stars yet?

Dear God, tell me you're not getting sucked into all that tourist bullshit."

"Mostly I've seen miles of freeway and the inside of my apartment."

"Well, that's just sad. Makes me even more glad that Carl dragged your skinny ass all the way out here tonight."

I've put on fifteen welcome pounds since the years when my mother monitored every tiny thing that went in my mouth, and while I'm perfectly happy with my size-eight ass, I wouldn't describe it as skinny. I know Evelyn means it as a compliment, though, and so I smile. "I'm glad he brought me, too. The paintings really are amazing."

"Now don't do that—don't you go sliding into the polite-conversation routine. No, no," she says before I can protest. "I'm sure you mean it. Hell, the paintings are wonderful. But you're getting the flat-eyed look of a girl on her best behavior, and we can't have that. Not when I was getting to know the real you."

"Sorry," I say. "I swear I'm not fading away on you."

Because I genuinely like her, I don't tell her that she's wrong—she hasn't met the real Nikki Fairchild. She's met Social Nikki who, much like Malibu Barbie, comes with a complete set of accessories. In my case, it's not a bikini and a convertible.

Instead, I have the *Elizabeth Fairchild Guide for Social Gatherings*.

My mother's big on rules. She claims it's her Southern upbringing. In my weaker moments, I agree. Mostly, I just think she's a controlling bitch. Since the first time she took me for tea at the Mansion at Turtle Creek in Dallas at age three, I have had the rules drilled into my head. How to walk, how to talk, how to dress. What to eat, how much to drink, what kinds of jokes to tell.

I have it all down, every trick, every nuance, and I wear my practiced pageant smile like armor against the world. The result being that I don't think I could truly be myself at a party even if my life depended on it.

This, however, is not something Evelyn needs to know.

"Where exactly are you living?" she asks.

"Studio City. I'm sharing a condo with my best friend from high school."

"Straight down the 101 for work and then back home again. No wonder you've only seen concrete. Didn't anyone tell you that you should have taken an apartment on the Westside?"

"Too pricey to go it alone," I admit, and I can tell that my admission surprises her. When I make the effort—like when I'm Social Nikki—I can't help but look like I come from money. Probably because

I do. Come from it, that is. But that doesn't mean I brought it with me.

"How old are you?"

"Twenty-four."

Evelyn nods sagely, as if my age reveals some secret about me. "You'll be wanting a place of your own soon enough. You call me when you do and we'll find you someplace with a view. Not as good as this one, of course, but we can manage something better than a freeway on-ramp."

"It's not that bad, I promise."

"Of course it's not," she says in a tone that says the exact opposite. "As for views," she continues, gesturing toward the now-dark ocean and the sky that's starting to bloom with stars, "you're welcome to come back anytime and share mine."

"I might take you up on that," I admit. "I'd love to bring a decent camera back here and take a shot or two."

"It's an open invitation. I'll provide the wine and you can provide the entertainment. A young woman loose in the city. Will it be a drama? A rom-com? Not a tragedy, I hope. I love a good cry as much as the next woman, but I like you. You need a happy ending."

I tense, but Evelyn doesn't know she's hit a nerve. That's why I moved to LA, after all. New life. New story. New Nikki.

I ramp up the Social Nikki smile and lift my

champagne flute. "To happy endings. And to this amazing party. I think I've kept you from it long enough."

"Bullshit," she says. "I'm the one monopolizing you, and we both know it."

We slip back inside, the buzz of alcohol-fueled conversation replacing the soft calm of the ocean.

"The truth is, I'm a terrible hostess. I do what I want, talk to whoever I want, and if my guests feel slighted they can damn well deal with it."

I gape. I can almost hear my mother's cries of horror all the way from Dallas.

"Besides," she continues, "this party isn't supposed to be about me. I put together this little shindig to introduce Blaine and his art to the community. He's the one who should be doing the mingling, not me. I may be fucking him, but I'm not going to baby him."

Evelyn has completely destroyed my image of how a hostess for the not-to-be-missed social event of the weekend is supposed to behave, and I think I'm a little in love with her for that.

"I haven't met Blaine yet. That's him, right?" I point to a tall reed of a man. He is bald, but sports a red goatee. I'm pretty sure it's not his natural color. A small crowd hums around him, like bees drawing nectar from a flower. His outfit is certainly as bright as one.

"That's my little center of attention, all right,"

Evelyn says. "The man of the hour. Talented, isn't he?" Her hand sweeps out to indicate her massive living room. Every wall is covered with paintings. Except for a few benches, whatever furniture was once in the room has been removed and replaced with easels on which more paintings stand.

I suppose technically they are portraits. The models are nudes, but these aren't like anything you would see in a classical art book. There's something edgy about them. Something provocative and raw. I can tell that they are expertly conceived and carried out, and yet they disturb me, as if they reveal more about the person viewing the portrait than about the painter or the model.

As far as I can tell, I'm the only one with that reaction. Certainly the crowd around Blaine is glowing. I can hear the gushing praise from here.

"I picked a winner with that one," Evelyn says. "But let's see. Who do you want to meet? Rip Carrington and Lyle Tarpin? Those two are guaranteed drama, that's for damn sure, and your roommate will be jealous as hell if you chat them up."

"She will?"

Evelyn's brows arch up. "Rip and Lyle? They've been feuding for weeks." She narrows her eyes at me. "The fiasco about the new season of their sitcom? It's all over the Internet? You really don't know them?"

"Sorry," I say, feeling the need to apologize.

"My school schedule was pretty intense. And I'm sure you can imagine what working for Carl is like."

Speaking of ...

I glance around, but I don't see my boss anywhere.

"That is one serious gap in your education," Evelyn says. "Culture—and yes, pop culture counts —is just as important as—what did you say you studied?"

"I don't think I mentioned it. But I have a double major in electrical engineering and computer science."

"So you've got brains and beauty. See? That's something else we have in common. Gotta say, though, with an education like that, I don't see why you signed up to be Carl's secretary."

I laugh. "I'm not, I swear. Carl was looking for someone with tech experience to work with him on the business side of things, and I was looking for a job where I could learn the business side. Get my feet wet. I think he was a little hesitant to hire me at first—my skills definitely lean toward tech—but I convinced him I'm a fast learner."

She peers at me. "I smell ambition."

I lift a shoulder in a casual shrug. "It's Los Angeles. Isn't that what this town is all about?"

"Ha! Carl's lucky he's got you. It'll be interesting to see how long he keeps you. But let's see ... who here would intrigue you ...?"

She casts about the room, finally pointing to a fifty-something man holding court in a corner. "That's Charles Maynard," she says. "I've known Charlie for years. Intimidating as hell until you get to know him. But it's worth it. His clients are either celebrities with name recognition or power brokers with more money than God. Either way, he's got all the best stories."

"He's a lawyer?"

"With Bender, Twain & McGuire. Very prestigious firm."

"I know," I say, happy to show that I'm not entirely ignorant, despite not knowing Rip or Lyle. "One of my closest friends works for the firm. He started here but he's in their New York office now."

"Well, come on, then, Texas. I'll introduce you." We take one step in that direction, but then Evelyn stops me. Maynard has pulled out his phone, and is shouting instructions at someone. I catch a few well-placed curses and eye Evelyn sideways. She looks unconcerned "He's a pussycat at heart. Trust me, I've worked with him before. Back in my agenting days, we put together more celebrity biopic deals for our clients than I can count. And we fought to keep a few tell-alls off the screen, too." She shakes her head, as if reliving those glory days, then pats my arm. "Still, we'll wait 'til he calms down a bit. In the meantime, though ..."

She trails off, and the corners of her mouth turn down in a frown as she scans the room again. "I don't think he's here yet, but—oh! Yes! Now *there's* someone you should meet. And if you want to talk views, the house he's building has one that makes my view look like, well, like yours." She points toward the entrance hall, but all I see are bobbing heads and haute couture. "He hardly ever accepts invitations, but we go way back," she says.

I still can't see who she's talking about, but then the crowd parts and I see the man in profile. Goose bumps rise on my arms, but I'm not cold. In fact, I'm suddenly very, very warm.

He's tall and so handsome that the word is almost an insult. But it's more than that. It's not his looks, it's his *presence*. He commands the room simply by being in it, and I realize that Evelyn and I aren't the only ones looking at him. The entire crowd has noticed his arrival. He must feel the weight of all those eyes, and yet the attention doesn't faze him at all. He smiles at the girl with the champagne, takes a glass, and begins to chat casually with a woman who approaches him, a simpering smile stretched across her face.

"Damn that girl," Evelyn says. "She never did bring me my vodka."

But I barely hear her. "Damien Stark," I say. My voice surprises me. It's little more than breath.

Evelyn's brows rise so high I notice the movement in my peripheral vision. "Well, how about that?" she says knowingly. "Looks like I guessed right."

"You did," I admit. "Mr. Stark is just the man I want to see."

I hope you enjoyed the excerpt! Grab your own copy of *Release Me* ... or any of the books in the series now!

The Original Trilogy
release Me

claim Me

complete Me

And Beyond...
anchor me

lost with me

enchant me

novellas
take me

have me

play my game

seduce me

unwrap me
deepest kiss
entice me
hold me
please me
indulge me
cherish me

ABOUT THE AUTHOR

J. Kenner (aka Julie Kenner) is the *New York Times*, *USA Today*, *Publishers Weekly*, *Wall Street Journal* and #1 International bestselling author of over one hundred novels, novellas and short stories in a variety of genres.

JK has been praised by *Publishers Weekly* as an author with a "flair for dialogue and eccentric characterizations" and by *RT Bookclub* for having "cornered the market on sinfully attractive, dominant antiheroes and the women who swoon for them."

A six-time finalist for Romance Writers of America's prestigious RITA award, JK took home the first RITA trophy awarded in the category of erotic romance in 2014 for her novel, *Claim Me* (book 2 of her Stark Saga) and another RITA trophy for *Wicked Dirty* in the same category in 2017.

In her previous career as an attorney, JK worked as a lawyer in Southern California and Texas. She currently lives in Central Texas with her husband, two daughters, and two rather spastic cats.

Stay in touch! Text JKenner to 21000 to subscribe to JK's text alerts. Visit www. jkenner.com for more and to subscribe to her newsletter!